# WINTER
# ROAD

# ALSO BY JOANNE DEMAIO

**The Winter Novels**
*Snowflakes and Coffee Cakes*
*Snow Deer and Cocoa Cheer*
*Cardinal Cabin*
*First Flurries*
*Eighteen Winters*
*Winter House*
*Winter Road*
*—And More Winter Books—*

**Beach Cottage Series**
*The Beach Cottage*
*Back to the Beach Cottage*

**Standalone Novels**
*True Blend*
*Whole Latte Life*

# ALSO BY JOANNE DEMAIO

**The Seaside Saga**
*Blue Jeans and Coffee Beans*
*The Denim Blue Sea*
*Beach Blues*
*Beach Breeze*
*The Beach Inn*
*Beach Bliss*
*Castaway Cottage*
*Night Beach*
*Little Beach Bungalow*
*Every Summer*
*Salt Air Secrets*
*Stony Point Summer*
*The Beachgoers*
*Shore Road*
*The Wait*
*The Goodbye*
*The Barlows*
*The Visitor*
*Stairway to the Sea*
*The Liars*
*—And More Seaside Saga Books—*

Copyright © 2023 Joanne DeMaio
All rights reserved.

ISBN: 9798399947617

Joannedemaio.com

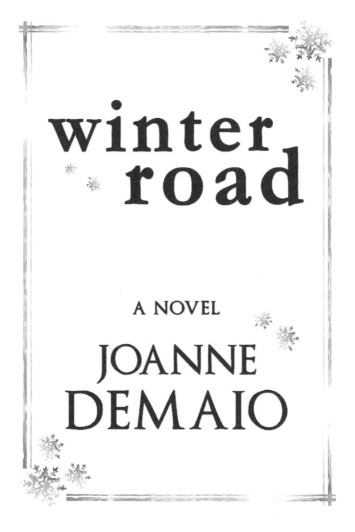

# winter road

## A NOVEL

## JOANNE DEMAIO

# *one*

LAZY SNOWFLAKES TUMBLE AND SPIN from the dark sky. It's as though someone's shaking a snow globe over the town of Addison's Main Street tonight. In the glow of colonial-style lampposts, those snowflakes swirl. But the gentle sight doesn't match what Faye Weston's feeling. She wishes it did. Hurrying along the cobblestone sidewalk, Faye wishes *she* felt as light and carefree and filled with a dusting of hope.

Instead, the snowy scene makes her sad.

"Listen, Dad," Faye says to her father beside her. "I don't much feel like celebrating right now."

Her father turns up the collar of his coat. "But it's New Year's Eve, Faye. Come on," he encourages. "Things will look up when we get there. You'll see."

And she does see. On The Green across the way, Faye sees more snowcapped lampposts wrapped in twinkling garland and topped with balsam wreaths. Burgundy velvet

1

bows on those wreaths flutter in the wintry breeze. The town Christmas tree glimmers in colored lights, too. Then there's the coffee shop and the general store up ahead. Shining ornaments hang in their windowfronts lined with cottony faux snow. And on those cobblestone sidewalks, people bundled in coats and scarves bustle past. Couples walk arm in arm; friends talk close—their heads dipped against the falling snow, their shoulders hunched against the cold.

Finally, Faye and her father approach Joel's Bar and Grille. It's discreetly tucked into a brick building. But red neon bells flashing in the front window give away the merriment inside. As her father opens the tavern's heavy wooden door, a waitress hands him a decorative whisk broom. The stiff corn bristles are golden; the mini broom's handle is wrapped in blue twine.

"We'll be sweeping out the old year at midnight!" the waitress explains.

Faye gives a small smile, then looks back over her shoulder when a distinct sound outside gets her attention. A horse-drawn sleigh is circling The Green. Silver bells on the horse's harness jingle in the night. Faye also sees the old saltbox colonials and turreted Victorians and gabled English Tudors surrounding The Green. The houses are aglow with lamplight and candles in the windows.

Oh, that quintessential New England sight says nothing more than home.

Which makes her heart sink—knowing she just lost her own.

"Check, check and check," Joel Briggs quietly says. As the owner of Joel's Bar and Grille, he's making the rounds before the festivities swing into high gear. White linens drape over square tables set on the wide-planked wood floor. All the black Windsor chairs have been polished. Brass picture lamps shine on framed oil paintings of schooners and ship captains. Coach-light sconces glimmer on the dark paneled walls. Silver and gold ornaments dangle from garland strung across the beamed ceiling. The bar's decorated, too, with miniature twinkling Christmas trees at either end.

And the place is mobbed.

But Joel has one last-minute task to attend to. He's standing inside near the six-panel wooden entrance door. Its brass door pull gleams. And through the door's paned sidelight windows, he sees snow falling outside. A familiar face approaches, too.

"Derek," Joel says, opening the door. His friend is coming in from the cold and pulling a wool beanie off his head.

"Hey there, Joel," Derek greets him. "Getting this old door ready for the big sweep-out?"

"You got it. Just oiling the hinges."

"Let me help with that," Derek offers.

"Thanks, man. Would you open and close it? Work in the oil?"

"Sure thing." Derek shoves his beanie into his jacket pocket and lends a hand. "Door looks a little different?"

"It is." While Joel's oiling its hinges, he explains. "Picked it up at the salvage yard last month," he says. "Door actually dates back to the colonial era." He pulls a

3

rag from his back pocket and gives the hinges a final buff.

"Great historic vibe," Derek tells him, keeping the door slowly swinging. "You do this ceremonial door-opening every New Year's. What an entryway you've got now."

"Yeah. The grand old door suits this building's history in town—including the stone hitching posts right outside. Those hail back to the days when ship captains hitched their *horses* there before coming in for ale and storytelling."

Derek nods. "Not much has changed, my friend, has it?"

The two men test the door once more to be sure it smoothly opens. When it does, Derek clasps Joel's shoulder. "Okay, Briggs. Now to find Vera."

"Enjoy yourselves," Joel says, turning back to the hinges.

But no other door prep can be done—not with more patrons arriving. Some are dressed in their finest formal threads—tailored suits and sequined dresses. Others are casual in jeans and sweaters. As they enter, a gust of cold, snowy air blows in, too. So for a few minutes, Joel stands just inside the entrance, lifts mini corn brooms from a massive basket and gives one to each customer. The whisk brooms are all decorated. Some of their short handles are hand-tied with yarn; some with braided hemp twine. Still others have looped leather-string handles. The bristles are natural on some; black on others; red on a random few.

And the lively remarks don't stop. There are comments, questions, familiar slaps on Joel's back. Handshakes, too.

*Hey, Joel! Getting those hinges greased for the big event?*
And, *Heavy new door, guy. Will the old doorstop keep it open later?*
And, *My favorite part of the year, sweeping out the old—right here!*
And, *What's with the whisk brooms, Briggs?*

Joel laughs and talks and explains. "Right at midnight, we ceremoniously open this big door. Grab our brooms and sweep out *all* the bad of the old year," he says, climbing a stepladder beside that door. "Then we welcome goodness into the new. Well, hope and pray for it, anyway," he adds while stringing a black-and-gold *Happy New Year!* banner above the massive door. Stepping off the ladder then, Joel straightens his black vest over his black pants. Shoves up his white button-down's shirtsleeves, too.

Finally, he's ready for the night to begin.

⁓

Brooms, brooms, brooms.

Everywhere there are adorable whisk corn brooms. From their booth, Faye notices them throughout the tavern. Her father's has braided blue twine zigzagging up the handle. Natural bristle brooms are propped on tables. From their leather handles, the little brooms hang on chairbacks. A woman at a nearby booth slowly spins her red-bristled mini broom on the tabletop. A guy at another table uses his ribbon-wrapped corn broom to keep beat to the jukebox tunes.

Of course, Faye notices them all because she's

glancing around—instead of eating. She only picks at the turkey-and-Swiss wrap in front of her.

"See?" her father prods. "Aren't you glad you came out to celebrate?"

"Celebrate?" She looks across the booth table at him. Her father's hair is more silver than black. He wears a dark sweater over a flannel shirt. And she can tell—he's just trying to help. "Celebrate what, Dad?" Faye quietly goes on. "Not much for me. Not this year, anyway. You know that. Because I lost my apartment in that beautiful historic home. Oh, how I loved it, too. Loved being on the third floor. Loved the vaulted ceiling. Those creaky floors and big, sunlit windows. The cozy alcove where I'd curl up with a book. The hissing radiators." She sighs now. Just sighs. "And then I spent Christmas week leaving it behind and moving back in with you."

"Well." Her father sips from his glass of beer. "Who could've known your landlord would stop renting the two units and move in extended family instead?" He pauses, tipping his head. "Now you see? Family moving in … the same way you did. With me."

Faye waves him off in the dark tavern. It's noisy with talk and merriment all around them. More holiday tunes play on the jukebox. Some folks sing along. "To top it off," she goes on, "the lease termination was so sudden. With hardly any notice! And the housing market is just crazy. I mean, there's *nothing* for sale—especially this time of year."

"Something will come up, sooner or later."

"Yep. And when it does, I won't stand a chance between the out-of-control home prices and two-income couples outbidding me as a single woman." She sits back, picks up her turkey wrap and sets it down without a taste. "So I'm just not feeling the holiday spirit this year."

"Faye," her father persists. "You've *still* got good things on the horizon. Like your new job."

It's true. She'll be starting work right after the holiday at Silver Settings, a Connecticut-based flatware company. Their cutlery designs are rooted in the finest New England traditions: timeless style, classic lines, enduring quality. Made in the USA, too—right here in Addison. It's a good opportunity for her. Faye knows it. And she was ready for a change in her life. Welcomed it, actually. The nice company, the nice people. Nice salary and benefits, too—which far surpass what she earned as a social media manager for a local insurance company.

Yes, she wanted something shiny and new and found it at Silver Settings. It all felt right—until she lost her home.

"Sorry, Dad," she says now, then sips her wine. "But when my new coworkers ask me about myself, what am I going to say? That I'm thirty-four years old and just moved back into my childhood home?"

"Well, that's common these days," her father counters. "Your coworkers will understand. Lots of people your age are living with their parents again. It's because of this darn real estate market that simply won't cool down."

"I know." She gives him a sympathetic smile, then lifts her honey-gold plaid jacket from the booth seat. Draping the wool jacket over her shoulders, she goes on. "This just isn't the New Year's plan I had in mind. And actually?" Faye pauses and looks around the busy bar. Each table is filled. More people sway on the dance floor to that jukebox's holiday music. "Dad? I'm afraid, too."

"Afraid?"

"Of the new job, for one. I mean, was it a mistake? I was so comfortable where I was. And … And I'm afraid I'll *never* find a house now—with the way the market's turned. So I'm back home, and another fear comes with that."

"Like what, Faye?"

"Like … how can I meet anyone while living at home? Not to mention …" Instead of going on, Faye first takes a long breath. "I really miss Mom," she says then. "I wish I could talk to her right now."

Her father nods. "Can't believe she's been gone three years already." He reaches across the table and squeezes Faye's hand. "But I'm here. And I want to help."

"Dad—"

"Listen. You might be surprised at what I can come up with," he interrupts. "Like …" he begins, then hesitates.

And Faye sees it. Sees that as he looks around the room, he's trying to think of *something* to lift her spirits. And she loves him all the more for it.

"Like … Like this," he goes on. "Let's allay those fears of yours. Got a pen?"

"Oh, no." Faye pulls a pen from her purse. "What are you up to?"

Her father grabs a few long, white napkins. "We can *make* this be a good New Year's, Faye. And here's how." He flattens a paper napkin and begins writing. "Your mother was such a list-maker," he says, scrawling out something. "And next year will be your thirty-fifth. So how about *this* list to guide you? It's something she might've suggested." He turns the napkin and shows his penned list title: *35 Things Before 35.*

"Oh my gosh! I don't know if I can think of *five* things, Dad!"

"Well … they can be big *and* little. Let's get some jotted down."

"You're just trying to distract me." Faye squints over at him while downing a few French fries. "*And* cheer me up."

"What's wrong with that? It's what dads do. So let's begin—your life list, we'll call it." He lifts his cheeseburger and takes a bite, then grabs up the pen again. "What are some things you'd like to do this year? *Little* things. Start small."

"Well," Faye begins. "A friend gave me a houseplant for Christmas. So …'" She takes the pen from her father.

And they begin. Her life list builds as they slide that pen back and forth.

Back … and forth.

First her idea … then his … over and over.

Hers: *Number 1. Don't kill a houseplant.*
His: *Number 4. Learn a new art form.*
Hers: *Expertly cook something—from scratch!*
His: *Drive a muscle car. Even for a day.*
Another his: *Number 9. Don't be afraid to say no to people.*
Hers: *Number 12. Learn to sew a button.*
His: *Smile more.*

And the scrawled entries go on …

9

His: *Number 14. Go fishing—at least once.*
Hers: *Learn a magic trick.*
His: *Run a 5K marathon.*
Hers: Crosses out *5K* and writes *2K.*
Hers: *Number 19. Buy a house!*
His: *Number 20.*

Her father pauses, then jots a few more words before turning the long napkin her way. "Now don't get mad at me for this one."

"Dad!" Faye says, reading his number twenty. "Fall in love?"

"Why not?"

"And on my first date, tell him ... what? That I live in my childhood home? With my father scuffing around in his slippers?" Faye shakes her head. "You can scratch that one for now, Dad. *Not this year,*" she murmurs. She notices, too, that he *doesn't* scratch that one. Instead he just flips the paper napkin over, then back to the front again.

"We're out of space. But that was a good start, Faye. You just keep adding to this list until you reach *thirty-five* goals." Her father pats her hand and gives her back the pen and list, too. "Look. It's almost time for the countdown," he says, nodding to the black pedestal town clock on the snowy green outside their window. "That clock will soon strike twelve."

Which does something to Faye. Seeing the very last minutes of this year tick away leaves her ... disappointed. Sad. Lonely, maybe. It's hard to tell which—but none of them feel good. So after tucking away her pen, she discreetly lifts that scrawled napkin to dab a tear. Excuses herself, too, telling her father she'll be right back before slipping out of the booth and getting lost in the crowd.

There's just enough time.

Joel rushed outside to his pickup truck parked on the street. He reaches for the last basket of whisk corn brooms and hefts the basket in his arms. His bartender, Kevin, said they need a few more brooms for late arrivals. Okay, *these* mini brooms are snow dusted, but will work just the same. On his way slipping along the cobblestone sidewalk, Joel looks twice at a woman outside the tavern's main entrance. Beneath a gold-plaid jacket draped over her shoulders, she wears a turtleneck sweater, brown corduroys and tall leather boots. Her blonde hair falls in a blunt cut to her shoulders. Long bangs sweep her eyes. Alone and standing off to the side, she's also dabbing a paper napkin to those partially concealed eyes.

"Hold those tears!" Joel says as he approaches the woman.

"What?"

"We're minutes away from the new year." Joel hurries closer. "So you just can't cry. You really have to save those tears for another day, because crying on New Year's is said to bring on a whole year of sadness." Quietly then, with concern, he goes on. "And I don't want that for you," he says around the basket in his arms.

"Well, I am upset," this woman reveals. "And I kind of *want* to cry—so I can't promise anything."

11

Joel shakes his head and sets the broom basket on the snowy cobblestones. "How about if I stand with you, then? Just for a minute to be sure you don't shed those tears."

"Really, you don't have to do that," the woman insists. But she holds that napkin at the ready. "I just needed a little air. I'm fine, though."

"Maybe. But I own the place and don't like to see my patrons upset. You sure you're okay?" He steps closer. She's cold. It's apparent by the way she hikes that plaid jacket up higher on her shoulders. "Anything I can do to help?"

She shakes her head. "I'll be all right. Someone's waiting for me inside."

"Not the reason for those tears, I hope?"

"No, not at all. It's my father in there. He brought me out tonight. And … Well, I don't want to bother you with my story."

"Bother me? Hey, it's a bartender thing—people unload on me." He tugs his black vest closed in the cold December air. "And listen, we have a tradition here at Joel's Bar and Grille. Every New Year's Eve, right at midnight, we sweep *all* the past year's troubles, problems, dust, bad memories—*whatever*—right out the propped-open tavern door. So I hope you'll partake. You know," he says, squinting through the snowflakes at her eyes, "*sweep* those pesky troubles away *instead* of crying about them. Did you get a broom?" He motions to the decorated whisk brooms spilling from the large basket. Each broom's corn bristles are intricately hand-tied. But it's the craftsmanship that makes each unique. Wrapped or braided or twisted twines or yarns or ribbons hold together the golden bristles of each and every corn broom.

She nods. "We got one when we arrived. My father has it inside." There's a smile on her face, then. A small one, but it's there. "The thing is? My troubles need more than a broom," she quietly admits, pressing that paper napkin beneath her eyes once more.

"Careful. There's some writing on that napkin. You'll get ink on your face."

"Oh!" The woman looks at the semi-wrinkled napkin. Tries to flatten it then, too. "My list," she's saying with a glance at him. "I was working on it inside. It's … a life list, kind of. Thirty-five things to do before I turn thirty-five."

"That doesn't sound sad." Joel watches her. Falling snowflakes dust her hair and settle on the plaid jacket loose on her shoulders. "Your list sounds intriguing, actually. So why the tears?"

"Because number nineteen might never happen." She looks from him to the napkin-list. Squints through the lightly falling snow, too, as she reads more. "Number twenty probably won't, either."

"Nineteen and twenty? Let me guess …"

"Joel!" a waitress calls from the front entrance door just then. "It's almost midnight. Kevin says he needs those extra brooms."

Joel looks from the waitress, to this list lady, and back to the waiting waitress. "They're right here," he tells her, bending for the basket of decorated whisk brooms.

"Good." The waitress steps outside. "I'll take them in."

As she reaches for the basket, Joel grabs a whisk broom from it. Its bristles are trimmed just so. Its brown braided-twine tie winds up and down the handle in a checkerboard pattern.

"And hurry up inside," the waitress is calling back as the entrance door closes behind her. "It's just about time!"

Joel takes a step toward the door, then turns to the life-list woman. She looks at him from beneath those long bangs sweeping her eyes. Right then, they *both* start to say something, but stop with a quick laugh. And it's late—the clock's ticking down on the old year. So Joel looks from his watch to the vintage wood door with its long brass door pull. He reaches for it, opens the door and motions for the woman to go inside.

"*Come on,*" he whispers encouragingly. As she approaches, he gives her the checkerboard-handled whisk broom. And as she steps with it into the rowdy tavern, Joel lightly takes her arm. "Hey. Be sure with that countdown, you sweep that sadness away." When she looks back at him through the shadows, he goes on. "At least for tonight, okay?" he tells her over the loud hum of voices inside.

She gives a nod, looking as though she wants to say more—but is interrupted.

"Yo, Briggs!" Kevin calls out. He's behind the bar and pointing to his watch.

But when this woman starts to bring that napkin to her eyes, Joel disregards Kevin and instead gives her a friendly reminder. "No more tears?"

"They're not," she says, slowly maneuvering through

14

the milling people. "I'm just pressing them back," she assures him over her shoulder. Gives a little wave then, too.

Which is when he simply loses her and that gold-plaid coat among the sequined dresses and velvet toppers, the suits and sweaters, the ponchos and shawls.

So that's it. No name. No exchange of numbers. The two of them just passed in the night, like two ships out on the dark Addison Cove.

But Joel thinks of her, still.

At least until the expectant crowd gets his attention. The room is *electric* with anticipation. Crystal glasses are raised. Laughs ring out. Someone stops the jukebox as the New Year countdown is set to begin. Joel takes his position at the closed, freshly painted, brass-handled, six-panel, antique wood entrance door. The lights are low in the tavern. When a small spotlight shines on that heavy wood door behind him, he calls out to the waiting patrons, "Get your brooms ready!"

He does more, too. As he gives the order, he looks for the sad lady with her blonde bangs and crumpled life list at the crowded tables.

"Ready to sweep out the old?" Joel calls then. When he does, a muffled roar rises from everyone at the tables and long bar.

At Kevin's signal, Joel begins the countdown.

*"Ten … Nine."* In an exaggerated motion, he takes hold of the door's brass handle.

*"Eight … Seven."*

The entire tavern joins the chant then, with a random whistle or two cutting through the shadows.

*"Six … Five … Four."*

In the glow of the wall sconces' low light, he sees people prepping their corn brooms. They hold them over their tabletops. Prop them on the bar. Bend and hover them over the wide-planked wood floor. At the jukebox, people hold their braided and decorated mini brooms ready. Folks are even about to sweep the windowsills.

But Joel can't spot the lone lady in a gold-plaid coat.

*"Three."*

A palpable undercurrent pulses through the room.

*"Two."*

More whistles. Some hoots and hollers.

*"And … one!"*

With that, Joel swings open the grand tavern door. As he does, a chorus of cheers and *Happy New Year!* rings into the night—all as the old year gets brushed right out the door of Joel's Bar and Grille. There's a blur of golden corn bristles as tabletops are swept. Around beer mugs and wineglasses, the bar is brushed. Windowsills are swept. The jukebox, too. Corn broom bristles sweep across chairs and walls and frames of oil paintings and even the wide-planked wood floor. All the little braided and yarn-wrapped handles are gripped as the mini brooms *sweep-sweep-sweep*.

Out they go! All the old-year grievances *whoosh* toward the heavy wooden door Joel's holding open.

Out it all goes—the bad and sad and frustrations and disappointments.

Out the door and into the dark night they fly among snowflakes swirling on a winter breeze.

No one would know it, but all the while Joel does

16

something else, too. He keeps an eye out for the sad list-lady. He's still wondering about her as he breathes the crisp winter air blowing in with the new year ... and can't help feeling a little sad himself.

# *two*

---

*— Eight Months Later —*
*September*

JOEL BRIGGS NEVER THOUGHT IT would turn into this.

When he lifted some large stones from the earth of his backyard last spring, it was only to plant a few shrubs. Not to build a stone wall.

But all these months later, after many weekends spent two-handedly hefting rocks with his brother, Brett; and after a friend donated *more* stones rescued from the foundation of a dismantled old house; and after many more summer evenings cobbling together the gray mottled rocks in the glow of the firepit—while roasting hot dogs and having a beer or two with the guys, or his father—it happened.

A genuine New England rock wall snakes along one side of his property now.

And it's almost done. Only a small pile of stones remains in his backyard. But once they're gone, the tinkering and shifting and adjusting will definitely be ongoing. Rock walls are that way—an evolving work of art.

Standing on his farmhouse's front porch, Joel sips his coffee and looks over to the wall. Maybe he'll add a stone or two before going to work. So, coffee in hand, he heads across the lawn. Doesn't make it to the wall, though. Not with the line of cars snaking down the street. They're stopped, bumper to bumper. From some, passengers have emerged and stand there, leaning against their cars. Inside others, people lean forward, craning their heads toward—yes, he should've known—the little two-story, peaked bungalow next door.

The one house on Winter Road that's come up for sale the entire year.

And by midmorning this September Saturday? A traffic jam. There'll be house showings all day. Every fifteen minutes, buyers will pull up, park in line at the curb and wait for their time slot.

As Joel looks that way, he notices his neighbor across the street. The fire marshal, Bob Hough, is drawn to the same, unbelievable sight.

"Day off?" Bob calls out as he walks over. He's got on a zip sweatshirt, jeans and construction boots—ready to tackle yard work, no doubt.

"Nah. Going in after my coffee." Joel holds up his steaming cup. "Got to do some paperwork."

"Then a late night ahead of you?"

Joel runs a hand down his unshaven jaw. "Well," he reasons. "Tavern's *open* till midnight. Kevin, my head bartender, covers the late shift and closes up. Managing the place, I usually clock out earlier. But *first*," Joel adds, motioning his coffee toward the cars snaking along, "let's see if I can even get out of my driveway."

"No kidding," Bob remarks. "Sheesh, I haven't seen this much traffic on Winter Road in all the years I've lived here."

They pause at Joel's split-rail fence and look over at the neighboring house. The olive-colored bungalow has several peaks on the front. Its board-and-batten siding runs vertically—except for in the peaks. There, it's horizontal. Large, multipaned windows and an entrance alcove add to the house's country aesthetic. Surely one of the potential buyers lined up will grab it.

"Can you believe this?" Joel asks, nodding to the busy street.

Bob shakes his head. "What a zoo."

"Seller's market, that's for sure. Tough time to be house-hunting."

"Glad me and Chloe remodeled our place a few years ago and stayed put. Better than that circus."

"Well," Joel says, turning back toward his rock wall now. "Looks like we'll be getting a new neighbor anyway."

"And soon! I hear you have to decide in *one* day. Make an offer—*fast*." Bob carefully starts crossing the street to his own yard. "Lots of pressure!"

"I couldn't do that," Joel calls back to him with a wave. "After a fifteen-minute showing? Pretty wild."

⁓

Faye's not sure where to look: at the utterly charming bungalow she dreams of calling her own, or at the long, long line of cars parked along the curb of Winter Road.

Looking at the *house*, she can just envision her life in it. Imagine it as home.

But looking at the *folks* in all those cars, she can gauge the *fierce* house-buying intent. And get some sense of the competition she's up against.

"Oh my gosh, Dad," she says from the car's passenger seat. "What am I going to do?" She leans forward for a better view of the country home. "I *really* like it. This could be the one!"

"Don't get your hopes up, Faye. You've been through this before," her father reminds her as he drives closer. "And how many of those houses went to someone else? Plus, you haven't even *seen* the inside yet."

"I know." She lifts round wire-framed sunglasses to the top of her head and peers through the windshield. "But the outside! And the road! It's so quiet here. And pretty!" Surrounding maple trees stand tall. The trees' foliage is tinged with yellow as fall nears. And at the big farmhouse just ahead, a stately fir tree towers in the front yard. "I'd be close to you, too," Faye muses. As her father inches the car forward, she scrutinizes the bungalow's yard next. "Looks *just* the right size. Not too big, not too small."

Her father looks over now. He points out the tired shrubs, and an overgrown rose bush against a white picket fence. "Curb appeal's *pretty* good. Landscape could use some tending, though. Some freshening up. Maybe paint the house's front door, too."

21

But they don't look long at the property. Instead, they're drawn to the potential buyers exiting and entering the house ahead of them. There are families and couples. Faces are serious. Hands clutch papers and cell phones. People look over their shoulders, then lean close to plot their next move.

"*It's just a mania*," her father whispers, shaking his head.

"Well, Dad. It's the end of September already. And here in Addison? Not much hit the market all summer long. So people are like … vultures! Descending on the house I can just *picture* myself in!" Faye slumps in her seat. "Oh, how can I even compete?"

"Listen. If you like it, go with your gut. Give your best and final offer, Faye."

Problem is, her heart sinks when she *wants* it to soar— all as their car moves closer. So from the front seat, she does some last-minute number crunching on a notepad.

"Okay, Dad," Faye says, looking up then. "It's our turn. We have fifteen minutes," she reminds him while getting out of the car. Golden morning sunshine falls on the peaked bungalow she already loves. A soft breeze rustles the leaves in the trees. Her senses soak it all in— with hope. After straightening the gray sweater vest over her white tee and faded jeans, she takes a shaky breath, too. "Fifteen minutes, and then *maybe* number nineteen will be checked off my life list."

# *three*

By WEDNESDAY, IT'S OVER.

After Joel ends his morning run on a nearby wooded trail, he jogs up Winter Road. Wearing side-striped, black jogger sweatpants and a loose black tee, he breathes the cool morning air. Squints through the misty September sunlight, too. Lawns are still dew covered. The day's early light, golden. And his sneakered feet pound the pavement, again and again.

But suddenly, his step slows.

Slows in disbelief.

Because a real estate agent is actually hanging a *Sale Pending* banner across the *For Sale* sign at the bungalow next door. Sold—in four days.

So Joel walks closer. "That was fast!" he calls to the agent.

"Under a week?" She gives a short laugh. "That's slow by today's standards!" she calls back with a friendly wave, then turns to her car.

Hands on his hips, Joel just stands at the bungalow's front lawn and eyes the olive-colored house. With its gabled peaks and pediment accents, it's stunning. And someone grabbed it. Shaking his head then, he turns and crosses his own lawn to his front porch. It's his usual cool-down spot, where he leans against a porch post and slows his breathing. Lowers his heart rate, too.

And today? He *still* eyes that bungalow across the yard.

*"Sold!"* he whispers. After a swipe at his perspiring brow—and one more glance at the bungalow—he heads inside for a shower. A business stop in town is on his agenda, then on to work.

❧

An hour and a half later, Joel Briggs is surrounded by gleaming silver.

Walls of it.

Walls painted silver.

And he stands on a silver-and-black-patterned rug.

Three wooden shelves stretching from corner to corner line the room, too. Shelves *also* painted silver.

But it's what's *on* those shelves that has his attention. Sample pieces of every flatware style imaginable are precisely and evenly lined up on each of those three long shelves. There are silver satin finishes and silver mirror finishes. European sizes and American sizes. Dinner forks and salad forks. Place spoons. Teaspoons. Knives. Simple and ornate, country and modern and historical— the stainless steel glimmers just the same. The silver pieces are teardrop shaped and wedge shaped, with scroll detailing and line detailing. Silver never took so many forms. The room practically spins with it all as he walks along each wall and considers the options.

"Welcome to Silver Settings," a woman's voice says behind him now. "Can I help you choose a design?"

"I hope so," Joel answers, turning to the woman there. She wears a loose black blazer over a silky white turtleneck and reddish-brown faux-leather pants. Her blonde hair is pulled back in a loose chignon; long bangs brush her eyes.

She promptly crosses the room and shakes his hand. "Faye Weston," she tells him. "I'm the design coordinator here. Which means I coordinate designs with our customers, as well as coordinate marketing campaigns with the design team."

"Joel Briggs," he says back. Slightly squints at her, too. There's something familiar about this Faye, though he can't place it.

"Pleased to meet you, Joel." Faye motions to the stainless-steel flatware displays. "Did you have something in mind?"

"I think so."

"For your home? Or a gift, maybe?"

Joel shakes his head. "For my business, actually." He looks from Faye to the seemingly infinite flatware choices. "I saw your ad in yesterday's *Addison Weekly*."

"Excellent," Faye says, watching him now.

"And that ad made me realize I'm in desperate need of new flatware. This would be a large order for a local tavern."

"Here in town?"

He nods. "Joel's Bar and Grille."

"Ah, yes." Faye gives him a quick smile and pauses for a second while watching him. "I'm familiar with it."

"So you know it's in a really old brick building, and … given the history of Addison, well I'm looking for styles with a *colonial* feel to them."

"Oh, we have lots of options." Faye sweeps across the showroom and picks up a sample knife. "Starting with A. This design has a slight curve to the handles." She picks up another sample. "And then there's B. This fiddleback shape is *very* versatile. It's suited to everyday use, or a more formal setting with fine china." And another. "Now C has a detailed scrollwork which gives it a *really* vintage feel." She stops, then. Stops and looks up at Joel. Her head's tipped; an eyebrow's raised beneath those bangs. "Anything speak to you?"

Joel turns up his hands. "A, B *and* C?" He looks from the samples she holds fanned out in her hands to the walls of silver.

"You seem overwhelmed."

"Is it that obvious?"

"Well, I can actually bring sample place settings *to* the tavern. It really helps to see them in the environment where they'll be used. We can put them out on different tables. And under different light." Faye pauses a second, raising her head a bit and casting a long look at him from beneath those bangs. "It really does help."

"Huh. Heading over here this morning, I actually thought this would be easy."

Faye motions to him as she breezes out of the showroom. "Come to my office," she says over her shoulder. "I'll check my calendar and we'll schedule a time. I'll bring these and a few more designs."

So he follows her into her office—where there are more flatware samples lined across her desk. Boxes of flatware are also stacked on a three-tiered shelf on the wall. Amidst everything, a big window lets in lots of sunshine. Faye stands behind her desk and leans to her computer keyboard. Typing a few keys, she looks up at him waiting there. "Next Tuesday okay for you? If you work nights at the tavern, I *can* make an evening appointment."

"Days are better," Joel explains, drawing a hand down his jaw.

"You sure?"

He nods. "I own the place, and am more a manager than anything else. You know, handling the business end of things—orders, vendors, working with my brother on the books, managing the tavern and scheduling events. My day starts early and I'm usually *out* by five—except for busy times."

"Really! I just assumed, well, the business being a tavern and all."

"I do tend bar, too. Occasionally. But my head bartender, Kevin, is also my right-hand man. He usually closes up at night." Joel crosses his arms and leans against the doorjamb. "So an early appointment is better for me. Preferably before my lunch customers arrive. Say ... ten o'clock?"

"Perfect."

As Faye's inputting the details into her computer and printing a confirmation, Joel wonders what it is he still recognizes about her. "You seem familiar," he says then. "Have we met before?"

"Yes. I believe we have." Faye looks up at him again from beneath those long bangs. She slowly sits in her desk chair, too. "Unfortunately, it *wasn't* under the best of circumstances."

"Seriously?" He tips his head and scrutinizes her face, her hazel eyes, that thick blonde hair pulled loosely back.

As he does, Faye props her elbows on her desk and rests her chin on her clasped hands. "We met *at* your tavern, actually."

"We did?"

"Last New Year's Eve?"

"Wait a minute, wait." Joel steps closer to her desk. "You … you were the sad one."

"That's me."

"How do you like that. And did you hold those tears back?"

"I did," this Faye says with an easy laugh now. "So the year's been … okay. Things got better for me."

"Good. I'm glad, Faye." Still he scrutinizes her. "Wait. You had a list. A … *life* list, right?"

Faye nods and hands him his printed appointment confirmation. "Thirty-five things to do before I *turn* thirty-five."

"And you've been checking them off?"

"That's number one," she admits, pointing to a healthy potted plant on the corner of her desk. "Keep a houseplant alive."

"Ha!"

Before he can say more, though, her phone rings.

"So we're all set for now?" Faye asks, her hand hovering over the desk phone.

"Yep. Catch you ..." Joel pauses, looking at his confirmation. "Next Tuesday," he says with a nod. "Good seeing you again, Faye."

In one sweeping motion, she gives a friendly wave, then lands her hand on the ringing phone.

And as he walks away, Joel catches some of her talk.

*Faye Weston.* A pause, then, *I've been waiting for your call!*

Which gets Joel to slow his step as he heads down a hallway toward the door outside. Faye's voice fades the further away he gets.

*I'm holding my breath ... Is it good news or bad?*

The thing is, Joel finds *he'd* like to know, too. What mysterious news would this Faye Weston be waiting for? But all he can manage is a glance behind him right before he pushes out the door—never learning the outcome of the call.

⤫

Sadly, it's a done deal.

Faye sits still for a long moment after hanging up the phone. Her office is quiet. And what she has to do now *won't* be easy. So she gets up from her desk and walks to her open office door. Silver Settings is located in a historic colonial home on a side street off of Main. What were once parlors and bedrooms centuries ago are now offices. The original living room and dining room are now combined into an elaborate showroom. But some of the home's vintage charm still abounds in the wide crown molding. And old fireplaces. And drafty paned windows. Voices come from the offices near hers now, so Faye quietly closes her door and returns to her desk. On the way, she lifts a half-filled watering can from the top of a cabinet and gives her plant a drink.

Blows out a breath, too, when she finally sits again.

Reality hit hard just now. And what's next is unavoidable. So she picks up the phone to make *another* call—this one to her father. He's a math teacher at the high school, and she knows he has a free period at this hour.

"Bad news, Dad," she says when he answers his cell.

"*Ach.* You didn't get the house."

"No. My real estate agent just called. There were nearly a *hundred* showings. And I was close, Dad, but *narrowly* outbid this time. So I hope you don't mind me sticking around longer."

"Mind? I love having you there. My house is your house, kid."

"Thanks, Dad." Faye stands and leans against the wall beside the window. She looks out as her father goes on.

"Don't you give up, Faye. Keep trying for a house. I know how important it is to you."

"But it's heartbreaking. And I *really* liked that country bungalow. It was small and manageable. And on *such* a nice street. The houses are all beautiful on that Winter Road. The farmhouses. And Craftsman styles."

"Just try to stay optimistic. Maybe it happened this way for a reason."

"Dad. This is the *third* time I've missed out on a house, and the *third* time you've said that. I don't know how much more of this I can take."

"What do you mean?"

"I mean, I get so hopeful—and then *all* hope gets dashed! I don't know. I give up for now. Maybe the market will change next year."

She wraps things up with her father when there's a tap at her office door. It slowly cracks open then, and a coworker pokes his head in.

"Design meeting's about to start, Faye. I'm trotting over to Whole Latte Life. You want something to eat?"

"I'm not really hungry. How about just a coffee?"

When he nods and rushes off to the local café, Faye looks around her office—the same spot where she arrived this morning with *so* much anticipation. This was going to be the day. The day she got a phone call that went a different way.

Now? Now she scoops up the newly designed flatware prototypes lined across her desk. Clutching them close, she heads to the conference room for her meeting.

# *four*

FRIDAY LUNCHTIMES ARE ALWAYS BUSY. So as Joel walks out of the back stockroom and crosses the tavern, patrons greet him. High-five him. Have a few words. Tell him they're glad to see the tree again.

The whole time, Joel winds his way around the square tables. Striped curtains are tied back over the paned windows. So sunshine streams in, casting golden light in the dark room. Vintage tin platters hang on the wall over the jukebox. A waitress is looping a garland of red and gold leaves along the half-wall near the bar.

And the tree is in Joel's hands. It's an artificial fir tree set in a galvanized tin pail.

"Little early for a Christmas tree, no?" a patron asks from his seat at the bar.

Joel looks over to see Harry Dane, owner of Dane's General Store. Harry's draping his zip sweatshirt over his stool-back, then shoves up the sleeves of a light flannel he's wearing.

"Good to see you, Harry," Joel says around the cumbersome three-foot tree he's holding. "You want lunch?"

"Yeah. I phoned in my order. Just waiting to pick it up."

"Got it." Joel shifts the tree in his arms. "By the way. This here's not a Christmas tree."

"Sure looks it."

Joel sets the tree beside a twig pumpkin on the far end of the bar. "This is something new we started last fall. I keep it up till New Year's. Around here, this is referred to as the Trouble Tree."

"Oh, this oughta be good, Briggs."

"Yep. I change up its look for the season. Starting with orange harvest lights now. And little acorn ornaments." Joel nods to a bowl of them on the bar.

Harry picks up one of the acorns. "Okay …"

"And you see, folks like yourself sit down, pick an acorn to represent your troubles, and tell those troubles to the bartender. Then you symbolically hang those troubles on the tree." As he says it, Joel reaches to the bowl for an acorn and loops its gold thread over the needles of a tree branch. "Hopefully," he goes on, turning to Harry now, "you leave the place feeling a little better. Between the food, the drink and the talk."

"Huh," Harry says. "You know something, Joel? You and I have a lot in common."

"How so?"

"My father—"

"Norm. Norm was a great guy."

"He was." Harry nods. "We all miss him. And Pop used to say that working the soda fountain in our general

33

store is a little like being a bartender. Somehow, people's secrets always come out." He turns up his hands then. "So we have that in common, you and me. We hear it all."

"Ain't that the truth." Joel brushes some tree dust off his black vest and white button-down. "I'll check on your lunch. What'd you order, guy?"

"Heck, I'll be at the store inventorying birdseed all afternoon. Got me the meatloaf sandwich with a side of onion rings. To go."

∽◦

The sound is rhythmic.

And comforting, Faye thinks, as she scrapes a bamboo rake over the fallen leaves. It's early still, the very end of September. But she knows her father likes to get a head start on the raking. So does Roxy, apparently. In the late-afternoon sunlight, the little collie-shepherd romps through a small pile of leaves.

"It was a slow Friday at the office," Faye tells her father now. "So I clocked out early to help get this yard work done."

Her father looks over from raking around a few shrubs. "Many hands make light work."

"And paws!" Faye watches the dog, tail wagging, burrow into more leaves. "Roxy, scoot!"

While the dog runs in a happy circle, Faye takes off her quilted barn jacket and sets it beside her phone on the picnic table. After picking up her rake again, she doesn't get in more than three pulls before that cell phone rings. So she scoops it up off the table.

"The buyers backed out," her real estate agent lets on—practically before Faye finishes her greeting. The agent's words come rapid-fire. "They knew that bungalow was just too small for their family, but they got caught up in the frenzy."

"So what are you saying?" Faye asks.

"They want to pass on the house."

"But they signed a contract!"

"True, but what are we going to do? Force them to buy a house that's not right? We're understanding and work with our clients. And, Faye? As the next highest bidder? It's a golden opportunity—for *you*."

"*What?*"

Her agent practically whispers the rest, as though the news is almost impossible to believe. *"The house is yours, if you want it. Can you come in tomorrow for the final paperwork?"*

Faye nearly collapses with relief as she sits at the picnic table. "Oh yes! First thing!"

And the first thing Faye notices after confirming a time and hanging up is that her father's eyes are misty. Even though he's smiling and congratulating her and setting down his rake and hugging her—all while saying he'll go get a celebratory pizza take-out dinner.

The thing is? His eyes are still misty an hour later as he's walking into the house with a pizza from Luigi's.

Well now. The one thing Faye didn't count on is this—the moment she buys a house being so bittersweet. Her father got used to her being around all year, after all. Got used to her helping with yard chores. Got used to trading off who would make dinner every day—him after getting off work as a math teacher? Or her, after a busy day at Silver Settings.

"We can *still* trade off dinners, Dad," Faye assures him around a mouthful of pizza. She lifts a napkin from the kitchen table and pats her mouth. "We're still in the same town, you know. I'll just be ten minutes away. So you'll come to *my* house now. Roxy, too."

Her father nods. And there it is again—his misty eyes.

So Faye gets up, walks around the table and hugs him. "Thanks, Dad. For all your help these past months."

"I'm really proud of you," he tells her, patting her hand on his shoulder. And when she sits again and lifts her pizza slice, he goes on. "You did it, Faye." He pauses for a bite of his own pizza. As he does, a gentle breeze ripples the kitchen curtains. The last bit of sunlight glints on the distant horizon outside. "You made number nineteen come true."

* * *

In no time, that Trouble Tree had customers lined up at the bar. All day Friday—and Saturday, too—woes have been shared. Random acorns already hang on the fir branches illuminated with orange twinkle lights. Oh, Joel's heard *everything*. From a losing-a-job misfortune ... to the tale of a conked-out lawn mower. The troubles kept coming. Everything from a couple of broken-heart love stories ... to someone's toaster being on the fritz.

Yes, that little tree is weighed down already.

So when Kevin arrives at the tavern for Saturday's night shift, Joel books it out of there and leaves the troubles behind. He gets home just after sunset, checks his mailbox at the curb and walks to his front porch. On the way, he straightens the scarecrow tied to his lamppost. Notices the empty bungalow next door, too. Some family must be happy to soon call it home.

It's the twilight hour now. The sky above is a deep blue-violet. But on the horizon, thin, wispy clouds are tinged orange by the setting sun's pale light. It's an hour when the barred owls start up—and tonight's no exception.

*Who-who. Who-whooo.* A pause, then, *Who-who. Who-whooo.*

Joel stops on his stoop and leans against a porch post to listen. The rich, throaty call is captivating. He scans the tall fir tree in his front yard for any sign of the bird. There are none, but the song continues in the shadows of twilight. The owl quiets, though, when a couple out for a walk approaches. Leaves crunch beneath their step, and they wave to him on the porch. Joel nods with a slight wave back.

Life, life all around him. He's a witness to it every day in his tavern. Here on his farmhouse front porch, too. Always. He sees it all. Hears it all.

Yep, he's the guy who's always there, lending an ear, hearing everyone's stories. Everyone's troubles. Yet he doesn't reveal his own—which is that maybe his life's gotten a little … still. Leaning against the porch post and watching the horizon darken, he thinks that he's thirty-eight years old already, and two long years out of a relationship now. His days are constant, though. Reliable. But he's got no list of things to do—like the quirky life list that Faye's got going on. *And* seems to enjoy. Even just watering a houseplant is significant for her.

*Who-who. Who-whooo,* calls the owl in the night.

So, okay. Maybe he's worried. A little worried that ... this is it. He's watching it all in others' lives: anniversary toasts, stag parties, landmark birthdays. In his tavern, it all happens—life's milestones and celebrations.

He thumbs through his mail envelopes while still leaning there on the porch post. Still hearing the owl calls.

Even yesterday afternoon, Harry Dane mentioned an upcoming tux fitting. He'll be a groomsman at Derek and Vera's December wedding. Joel's own brother, Brett, is Derek's best man. Joel will be there, too—as a guest.

Which is how he feels lately. Like a guest witnessing everyone else's life.

*Who-who. Who-whooo* comes softer now, as though the owl's listening to his thoughts.

Which are that ... Truth be told, what's been shaping *his* life lately? As he turns to unlock his front door and go inside, Joel thinks something else, too. Thinks maybe he's actually afraid.

A little afraid that something has already passed him by.

# *five*

WHAT A DIFFERENCE A DAY makes.

A phone call makes.

A twist of fate makes.

A *house* makes.

As Faye wheels her mobile office wheelie-bag over the cobblestone sidewalks Tuesday morning, she feels *all* of that. Feels it so strongly that she has to actually stop—right there on the walkway—and look around. And enjoy her happiness.

Yes, over there. That's *her* town green now in its early October splendor, complete with brimming potted mums and golden foliage.

And that's *her* tall black pedestal town clock.

Because she did it. She signed the necessary papers on Saturday—and got the house on Winter Road. The charming olive-green bungalow with its roof peaks and cozy entrance alcove and little rickety picket fence? It's hers.

So she sees the town of Addison differently now. She sees it through pride of ownership.

But her days have been chock-full ever since. She bought the house on Saturday. And yesterday—Monday—she was stationed at Addison High School's gym for Career Day. Silver Settings' brochures were flying off the table; sample flatware was displayed; a poster hung behind her; and the students' talking was excited as they looked toward their future.

And now, Tuesday? This.

After pulling her wheelie-bag another cobblestoned block, Faye stops. Stops right at the heavy, black-lacquered wooden door of Joel's Bar and Grille. Her hand reaches for the antique brass door pull, and she steps inside. A scarecrow stands sentry there. Garlands of autumn leaves are strung across the shadowed, paneled room. Twig pumpkins flank the bar. Gourd centerpieces anchor the square tables.

Finally, she spots Joel. Dressed in black pants and a black vest with a white button-down beneath it, he's busy behind the bar. And that heavy door closes behind her as she walks toward him.

⁂

The noise does it.

That *thump-thump, thump-thump* gets Joel to turn. It's Faye. Dressed in a camel blazer over a fitted black top and black pants, she's got on a short leopard-print scarf, too. She's also pulling some hefty wheelie-bag behind her. Its wheels rhythmically thump over his wide-planked wood floors.

40

Joel checks his watch then. Ten o'clock—on the dot. It gives him an hour before he opens for the lunch crowd. So he nods, and shakes Faye's hand, and shows her the tables he's arranged for her flatware displays. "I kept the linens the same color on each," he tells her while walking across the room. "For comparison purposes, like you'd suggested."

"Excellent," Faye says while unbuttoning that camel blazer. She turns, then, to her wheelie-bag. From it, she lifts several boxes of flatware and explains each set while precisely arranging place settings on the tables. She's very focused. Particular, too—especially in the way she spaces out the pieces.

"We have to set them down *exactly* the same at each table. *Just ...* so," she's saying while lowering a spoon. "To compare the visuals the *exact* same way in your mind. Because ..." She takes another box of samples and moves to a second table. "By placing them *just* so—first there, then here, and over there—it helps. We can walk back and forth and carefully scrutinize them—"

"Just so," Joel says.

Faye looks over at him standing there, arms crossed, and watching her routine. She gives him a quick smile. "That's right," she agrees, then looks at the beautifully set table. "Just so."

She talks now about the historical influence on some designs; the mirror-finish on others. "Weight is important, too. So please pick up the pieces and simulate using them at a meal." As she says it, she—just so—picks up a fork and knife, joggles them, then simulates cutting food on a plate.

Joel follows her lead, sitting at one table, then another,

41

lifting a knife here, forks there, and … simulating.

"I did bring one modern style with a sleek, sophisticated look," Faye admits. "Just for comparison to the more traditional samples. But the modern set works well in *any* type of setting, so you *could* go with that."

She then explains the timeless *classic* look to the traditional styles. And how the colonial designs easily double for everyday use *and* formal. She talks about atmosphere, too, and how the soft lighting in the tavern enhances the stainless-steel's silver patina.

Joel considers each place setting. He moves from one table to the next. Steps back and eyes each flatware selection. Squints at them as he cuffs a white shirtsleeve. Asks a few questions, too, about the pieces' silhouettes. And about the size difference between European and American.

"Also, if you need more time," Faye tells him, "you can keep these for a few days. Get a second opinion? Maybe your wife would like to take a look?"

Joel glances up at her standing behind a black Windsor chair now and surveying the set tables. "Thanks anyway," he says. "But it's just me. I'm not seeing anyone. Not married, either—except to the tavern here."

"Oh. Okay, then."

So he turns to the tables and reaches for a particular fork. Its shape is influenced by an Old England style and has a clean look with no etchings on the pieces. "I'll go with this colonial design."

"Very nice choice."

"I think so, too, reflecting the history here. You know, the tavern's been in the family for decades. My father used to run it, and still lends a hand bartending. But he bought the place years ago because of its *historical* connection to old seafaring Captain Briggs and his family."

"Briggs?" Faye asks. She squints at him from beneath her long, blonde bangs. "Your ancestor?"

Joel nods. "And an important name in Addison. Captain Josiah Briggs, a prominent ship captain centuries ago, had two sons. One never made it back from sea. Another, Nathaniel, *did* safely return. He later took over the only tavern in town—which first opened in colonial times." Joel motions to an oil painting hanging on the wall. It's Nathaniel's stately framed portrait hailing from the 1800s. "Those days, after long seafaring journeys to the West Indies, the ship captains often stopped at the tavern upon their return. On their way home, a pitcher of ale and an evening of storytelling happened first. Their boots hit these old floors and their ocean tales spun out with each drink." Joel glances around the empty tavern. It's early, but the lunch crowd will be here soon. "A couple hundred years later and it's still the same."

"This place is very *rich* with history, then. I had no idea it was connected to your family."

"It is. You'll find a few Briggs landmarks throughout the town. Do you know that Lighting Lodge shop?"

"Yes!"

"It's housed in the home of Captain Josiah himself. And *here*," Joel explains, motioning to the tavern, "the building's exterior has been rebuilt, but some of the interior dates back centuries. The floors, some of the walls. Artwork. Those are the original hitching posts out front, too."

"Well, then. You've chosen an appropriately prominent style. It definitely suits the history of the place." Faye picks up his choice of pieces and says there's one more thing to do. "Because this large of an order will be a big investment for you? Let's look at them on the bar. To be certain of your selection."

Joel agrees and sets out a couple of plates, and glasses, and napkins.

And when they finish up and confirm the order, Faye packs up all the silverware.

"I really appreciate your help, Faye," Joel tells her. "Back at your showroom, all the silver just about blurred. What a difference seeing it here, on-site."

"Silver Settings is very accommodating. Thus … my mobile office," she says, tugging her wheelie-bag closer and pulling out a tablet computer now.

After noting how many settings he'll need, and confirming Joel's name and address and the total price, she tells him she'll email his receipt. "Also, all our products are made in the USA. Right here in Addison, actually. So I'm sure the sea captain's son—old Nathaniel Briggs—would approve."

"Absolutely."

"I'll check our inventory back at the showroom, but with such a large quantity, I doubt it will all be in stock. I'll call when it is—could be a couple of weeks. We're swamped, too, heading into the holidays." She tucks away her tablet, then snaps open her wheelie-bag handle. "But you're on the list!"

"Thanks again for coming out," Joel tells her.

"Oh, and here's my card with contact information.

You might think of some add-on pieces. Serving utensils. That sort of thing."

Joel reads the business card. "Faye *Weston. Weston …*" He looks at her then. "You any relation to Wayne? Lives in the old apple orchard development?"

Faye laughs. "That's my father! Do you know him?"

Joel nods. "From bingo at the church hall. I'm one of the callers there. Wayne, Pete. Gus and Hank. They always have a rowdy table."

Faye looks at him a second longer. Smiles and shakes his hand, too, before grabbing her wheelie-bag's handle and turning toward the door. "I'll let my dad know we're doing business."

⸙

On her way out, Faye notices something. The tavern is beautiful with its dark paneled walls and framed oil paintings and wide-planked wood floors. Linens cover the tables; sparkling glasses hang over the bar.

But what catches her eye is a charming artificial fir tree nestled in a galvanized silver pail. The whole thing sits beside a twig pumpkin right *on* the bar. Little country acorns hang from the tree's boughs. Tiny orange lights twinkle. "Great country-style Christmas tree, by the way," she says as she walks alongside the bar. "Getting to be that time of year."

"It's a tree of troubles, actually," Joel answers from behind the bar now.

Faye stops walking and turns back. "What?"

"It's not a Christmas tree," he explains. "It's the tavern's Trouble Tree."

She looks long at him. "Now I'm intrigued," she says, briefly taking a seat at one of the bar's stools. She reaches over and taps a few of the hanging acorns.

Joel walks closer and tells the story of the tree. Of how patrons confess a trouble or two while sitting at it. And how the hung acorns symbolize their troubles left behind. "So the Trouble Tree is actually a reminder that the tavern is a place where you can forget your problems for a while. Just hang them on the tree and free your thoughts. Relax," he says, picking up a damp cloth and wiping the bar top. "Talk, laugh. And leave here feeling a little ... lighter. With some hope, maybe."

"I've never seen anything like it," Faye says, spinning an acorn.

"Your father appreciated this tree when we started the tradition last year."

"My dad did?"

"Wayne occasionally told me some troubles on his mind." Joel pauses then. Pauses and just meets her eye. "One of them was a daughter he worried about," he admits. "I never realized it was you."

"Me? He mentioned me?"

"Little bit."

Faye gathers her things and stands to leave. And hesitates. And looks again at Joel. His face is shadowed in the tavern lighting; his dark eyes watch hers. "Last year was rough, to be honest," she lets on while buttoning her blazer.

He gives an understanding nod. "Here. I'll see you out."

"Okay," she says, picking up the handle of her wheelie-bag.

46

She and Joel cross the wide-planked floor then. After flipping the window *Closed* sign to *Open*, he gets the door for her.

"Thanks. And knock on wood," she tells Joel over her bag's thumping wheels, "my troubles are behind me now."

# *six*

FAYE'S DAYS FLY BY LIKE the swirling New England leaves.

The past two weeks were filled with mortgage appointments, phone calls, home inspections. Contrary to what other buyers have been doing, she wasn't about to waive an inspection in hopes of clinching a rushed sale.

She's also been getting moving cartons and bubble wrap and packing up at her father's.

And calling the moving company to confirm Saturday's move-in day. Her father graciously let her store all her furniture in the extra bay in his garage. Some pieces are in his basement, too.

And she's been filling out change-of-address forms.

And calling utility companies.

Not to mention, the holiday flatware orders at work have kept the clock hands spinning around.

Next thing Faye knows, it's mid-October. Her house

closing is only days away. So amidst the chaos, she's glad for an evening of calm—thanks to her life list. It's Monday, which means it's Calligraphy Night at the local art gallery. And as she works on number four on her list—*Learn a new art form*—everything beautifully slows.

Now there is only this.

This dipping her nib into the inkpot.

This perfecting her pen angle.

This repeating, repeating, rows of letters.

Ascenders: h and l.

Descenders: g and p.

Concentrating on each separate stroke.

Upstrokes.

Downstrokes.

Getting them ... just so.

Her hand works diligently. Every curved stroke is made with thought as she bends over her paper. The room is quiet. Several students are spread out at one long table. Voices are hushed as the precision of the craft is carefully sought. Sometimes there is only the soft scratch of pens on paper.

But suddenly, there's more.

There's the vibration of a text message arriving on Faye's silenced cell phone. She pauses, pen raised, and slides her phone close. The message is from a new friend, Sadie Welles. She met Sadie, Addison's event planner, this summer while signing up to give historical walking tours. Yes, another life list item accomplished: *Number 26—Join the community.*

*Need a favor,* Sadie's message reads. *You free for ice cream at the soda fountain?*

Faye taps out an answer. *Yes. Calligraphy class just about done.*

And from Sadie: *Perfect. Meet me at general store. See you at the counter.*

⁂

Everything at Dane's General Store is pumpkins, and wooden *Hello Fall* signs, and garlands of rust-colored berries, and illuminated twig wreaths, and bumpy gourds of greens and yellows stacked on mini hay bales.

All of it, every bit, Faye can just *picture* in her new home.

She tells Sadie this as they sit on swivel stools at the store's soda fountain. While spooning hot fudge sundaes, the two of them catch up.

"Harry and I are going to a costume party later this month. But … that's not why I texted you," Sadie says now.

"You mentioned a favor?" Faye asks, lifting a fudge-laced spoonful of ice cream.

Sadie nods and tells her that one of her tour guides, Lorrie, isn't available. "Just for one week, early in November. Lorrie gives the evening tours. And I know you do weekend tours, but I'm trying to lock someone down—*just* to fill in."

"Go ahead and sign me up! I'll be settled with the new house by then and can help you out."

"Oh, you're the best, Faye," Sadie says. She gives her Lorrie's brochure with all the historic Addison tour stops to cover. "I'm so glad I can count on you." Sadie's distracted then by Harry walking by. "Um, Mr. Dane?" she calls in a flirty voice while pointing to her paltry ice-cream dish. "Skimped much on my hot fudge?"

Harry gives her a wink and asks her to wait a second. When he returns, it's with a full *cup* of hot fudge in one hand and a cup of cookie dough bites in the other. The three of them talk then—until another customer motions Harry away.

"Good luck with your move Saturday, Faye," Harry calls back to her.

"You must be *so* excited," Sadie says. "Let's get some pumpkins out front. Harry has some for sale on that little pumpkin cart. Did you see it?"

"The one with the big wagon wheels and black-and-white striped awning?" Faye's asking as she's already grabbing her long cabled cardigan from the stool beside her.

Sadie nods as they cross the creaking wood floor. "We'll have a jack-o'-lantern night and decorate your stoop after you move in."

And by the time they pick out squat orange pumpkins and set them on the scale at the checkout, Faye can already picture her carved jack-o'-lantern twinkling in the night out on Winter Road.

❧

Tuesday morning, Joel stands in the lobby of Silver Settings. The walls around him are covered with black-and-white photographs. Each framed image visually tells a story of the company. There's the original three-story brick factory building. Chimney stacks rise from the roof; the paned windows are open for ventilation. Women work carefully at old polishing machines. Another woman in a short-sleeve blouse and checked skirt sits at a table where flatware pieces are laid out. The woman wears white gloves as she individually wraps each piece before packing them. Her gloves, according to the picture's caption, keep fingerprints off the shining silver flatware.

"A practice we still do today," Faye Weston says as she breezes in the entrance door. She tugs along her wheelie-bag and heads to her office. "I'll be right with you, Joel," she calls back.

"No rush," he answers, turning again to the vintage images.

Moments later, Faye's in the lobby with him. "I just got back from a wedding consultation," she says. "We provide rental flatware for special events."

"A wedding?" Joel turns to her. Faye's wearing a brown plaid blazer with matching pants. A wide brown suede belt wraps around her waist. Her blazer sleeves are folded back; a thick gold bangle is on her wrist. And though her blunt-cut blonde hair falls to her shoulders, she sweeps aside long bangs as she stands there. "Would that be Derek and Vera's wedding by any chance?" he asks.

"Yes! I just met with Vera."

"My brother, Brett, is married to her sister, actually. Brooke."

"Oh, so you'll be at the wedding?"

"I will."

Faye gives him a warm smile as she walks behind a

customer counter. "Should be a very nice affair," she says while shifting the many boxes of his new stainless-steel flatware.

They verify his order then. Faye opens a box and confirms the colonial style. She meticulously sets out a setting on a placemat with a dish. She also shows him the serving pieces he'd added on.

"And I'm including this with your order," Faye continues. She lifts a set of flour-sack blue buffalo-plaid kitchen towels. "They're complimentary," she adds, folding them into a bag. "So I think you're all set now. And we *do* thank you for your business, Mr. Briggs."

As she's processing his final payment, Joel gathers the boxes together. "So," he says, looking over at her. "How've you been? Since we last talked."

"Never better, actually." Faye hands him his receipt and a glossy flatware brochure. "I've had some good news since then."

"Really?"

She nods. "About a big one on my life list. Number nineteen."

"Now … I remember you mentioning nineteen last New Year's Eve. Nineteen and twenty, I think?"

"That's right."

"So what's number nineteen?" he asks while folding his receipt and paperwork into the towel bag.

"Number nineteen is why I was actually in tears that night at your tavern. I'd recently lost my apartment in a big colonial and had to move back home with my father. But what I'd wanted was a house of my own … which didn't seem in the cards. Until … well, it's finally happening." She pulls an empty key ring from her blazer pocket. "I did it! Bought my first house. After the closing later this week, I'll have the key and can move in."

"Good for you. And congratulations," Joel tells her. "Will you be living here in Addison?"

"I will. It's a really charming house with a peaked front—almost a Craftsman style. There's a great entry alcove, too. And a pretty thicket of woods beyond the backyard. It's on Winter Road. The little bungalow down on the far end."

Joel steps back and turns up his hands. "You're kidding."

"Mmh ... no."

"I mean, well, you'll be my neighbor."

"What?"

"I live right next door to that bungalow."

"Get out! In the farmhouse? The taupe-colored one? With the big fir tree in front?"

"That's the one. Been there ten years now."

And by her smile as she talks, well, Joel can see how much this home purchase means to Faye. Because that smile is luminous as she tucks her hair behind an ear, and mentions how crazy it was battling the nearly one hundred showings and numerous offers on the house, and that she didn't actually get it until the first buyer backed out of the deal.

"And now I'm so happy to know ... this!" she says, grandly motioning to him. "It'll be nice seeing a familiar face around."

"Likewise," Joel tells her with a nod. "And, listen. I'm wishing you a *really* good life in that house," he says, shaking her hand. As he does, one of the customer service reps arrives to help carry his order out to his truck. "It was nice doing business with you, too," Joel tells Faye as he hefts a couple of the boxes off the counter now. "And welcome to the neighborhood, Weston," he calls back on his way out the door.

# seven

N-31."

Friday evening, Joel looks out at the many long tables arranged in the church hall. Each table is filled with bingo players. Bingo daubers are dabbing and dotting this number, that number. Cards are filling up with pink dots. Blue dots. Green dots.

*"Ennnn-31,"* Joel calls again. "And *everyone's* having fun!"

A few *whoops* ring out, but then silence falls as the players anxiously await the next number.

"O-63," Joel announces from his calling station.

"Bingo!" comes instantly back from Betsy, a regular in the crowd. After her bingo is verified, she approaches the front table to pick out her prize.

"When're you getting married, Joel?" she asks, stopping a moment to chat with him. "Handsome guy like you."

*"Ah,* Betsy." Joel winks at her. Betsy looks to be in her

late seventies. Her short silver hair is layered. Over her black slacks, she wears a pale blue sweatshirt screen-printed with butterflies. "I only have eyes for you, hon. You know that."

She smiles and waves him off, but looks back at him as she heads to the prize table.

"Just say the word, Betz, and wedding bells will ring," he calls after her. A brief round of applause rises with his proclamation.

The games go on, then. A vertical-line regular bingo. A four corners—won by Gus when Joel calls, *"Ohhh-75 ... Give a little jump an' jive!"*

"What are you doing here on a Friday night, Joel?" gruff Gus asks on his way to the prize table. "You should be at the Apple Festival with a girl. Have a piece of pie. Take a spinning ride. Aren't you seeing anyone?"

*"Me?"* Joel motions to Gus' cap. "Popular guy like you with that jaunty tweed cap of yours, *and* as driver of the legendary Holly Trolley? *You're* the one who should have a nice lady on your arm, right here at bingo."

Gus waggles a finger at him. "You sly fox," he says, claiming his prize.

Next game up is a letter X bingo, during which a fake bingo is called—much to many *boos* from the tables.

Joel calms the crowd. "Easy does it, folks ... Susan just missed a number."

And when Susan *really* wins after two more numbers—B-14 and I-30—Joel escorts her to the prize table. Does a little step dance with her on the way and gives a spin that gets her long dress twirling, too.

"Okay, folks," he announces back at the calling station. "One more round, then a snack break. Next up?

Capital I. Straight across the top row horizontally, the very bottom row horizontally, and down the center row vertically. And away we go," he calls out as the evening ticks past. His amplified voice fills the vast hall for another hour. "N-42. *Ennn-42*, let's boogie on through."

⁂

Late Saturday morning, Joel actually makes it to the Apple Festival at the cove park. And with a girl, no less—his beautiful toddler niece, Harriet. His brother, Brett, chows down on a country-fair corn dog while Joel pushes the stroller. They walk past spinning wheels-of-chance games, all while Brett tells him that Brooke's selling mini apple-crumb cakes and caramel-apple cookies at the Snowflakes and Coffee Cakes booth.

And when they walk among whirling carnival rides, Brett mentions how his accounting firm took on two new business clients this week.

And when Brett takes little Harriet with him on the merry-go-round, Joel walks with the stroller past the towering Ferris wheel. Its reflection glimmers on the glassy cove waters this mid-October morning. Once Brett and Harriet catch up with him, they wander closer to the local business tents.

"Your new neighbor move into that bungalow yet?" Brett asks after settling Harriet in the stroller and pushing it along.

"I think it happens today."

"Who is it? A family? Older couple?" Brett asks. "Or your worst nightmare."

"Ha! None of the above, bro. It's a woman named Faye. We actually met when I ordered new flatware for the tavern. She works at Silver Settings."

"She downsizing, this lady?" Brett asks while eyeing a snowblower in a nearby vendor tent. "Empty-nest situation?"

"Far from it." Joel stops and eyes the same snowblower. It's a super-heavy-duty self-propelled model with wide clearing capacity. "She's in her thirties and just starting out with her first home."

Brett looks from the snowblower to Joel beside him. "Hey, hey, guy," he says, giving him a shove. "She available?"

"Who knows?" Joel answers. "She could be seeing someone. And she's *way* too beautiful, anyway. Totally out of my league. Not to mention, she'll be my *neighbor*. So I'm *not* going there."

"I guess." They start walking again. Brett pushes the stroller as they wind their way through the fair crowds. "It's just that it's been two years since you and Denise called it quits, so I just thought …"

"Yeah, and quit thinking," Joel says, shoving his brother this time. "Because if things don't work out with a *neighbor*—"

"Then your home life's wrecked."

"Exactly." Joel veers toward the craft tents now. "I'm just glad to have someone decent next door. And I want to welcome her to the neighborhood … maybe pick up a gift here."

"So what do you give for a new house?" Brett points to a nearby booth. "There's a fudge tent."

"Nah. No food."

"How about ..." Brett suggests while scoping out the tents, "embroidered linens? Or there, berry wreaths."

"Eh. Maybe those," Joel says, veering left. "Candle centerpieces."

"I'll leave that to you." Brett does a U-turn with the stroller. "Because I'm grabbing some free coffee cake from Brooke. You coming?" he asks over his shoulder.

"No. I'll see you around." But before he heads off, Joel gives little Harriet's hand a friendly tap.

It doesn't take long then. Joel strolls past only two booths. The first one is filled with monogrammed coffee mugs. He keeps walking. But at the very next booth, he stops.

And looks at the merchandise selection nicely arranged there.

And steps closer.

He eyes one item—and looks no further.

"Perfect," he tells the vendor. "That's it."

# eight

IT WAS AS BEAUTIFUL AS Faye had hoped.

The next week, on an unseasonably warm Saturday—three days before Halloween—her housewarming party guests arrived. They ate. They talked. They carved pumpkins. And they lingered into the evening on her deck. Now, after waving everyone off, she glances at an extra invitation left behind. The party certainly lived up to what she'd penned in her new calligraphy.

### Please Come:
*Housewarming and Jack-o'-Lantern Party*
*At my new home on Winter Road!*
*Dinner and pumpkins provided.*

Harry and Sadie are last to drive away—with a friendly horn-toot. Still clutching that invitation, Faye crosses her arms in her entry alcove and watches them leave.

Coworkers were here. Some old friends. Her father. He kept things easy for all and brought buckets of fried chicken from Chuck's Chicken. Sides, too. Mashed potatoes and gravy. Corn niblets. Dinner rolls.

And everyone left with jack-o'-lanterns and smiles.

So now Faye arranges her own twinkling pumpkin beside a big potted mum on her stoop. As she does, a voice calls out, *"Knock, knock!"* from the shadows. Straightening, she squints into the twilight and sees someone walking closer. He's wearing a canvas cargo jacket loose over black pants, a black vest and white button-down. And he's holding something large that she can't quite make out in the evening light.

⁓

"Joel!" Faye says as she steps off her stoop. "Too bad you missed it. I just had a housewarming pumpkin party." She motions to the jack-o'-lantern glimmering on the stoop of her bungalow. "You could've carved a pumpkin for your porch."

"You had a good day for it, nice and warm." Joel sees her in the lantern light of her stoop. Faye's burgundy cardigan is loosely half-tucked into skinny jeans. The jeans are tucked into black Chelsea boots; her blonde hair is twisted back in a low bun. "I just got home from work, actually. And hope you have room for another housewarming gift," he says, handing it to her.

"Aww. Thank you, Joel." Faye admires the long barnwood plank. The word *WELCOME* is painted vertically on the rustic wood. "This is just gorgeous," she adds while propping the sign beside her front door.

"I got it at the Apple Fest last weekend. Went there with my brother and his daughter. My niece, Harriet."

"Oh, that was my move-in day."

"How'd it go? Okay?"

"Smooth as can be." Faye sits on one of her stoop steps. She loops her hands over her knees, too, and looks up at him. "Busy, though."

"I'll bet. Getting settled in?"

"I am." She pats the wide step where she sits. "Here. Sit and talk a bit, neighbor."

"If I'm not keeping you."

"No. It's such a nice evening," she says, motioning to the stars emerging in the midnight-blue sky. "Tell me a little about the neighborhood?"

Joel looks long at her, then nods. Sits on that wide stair with her, too. He doesn't say anything for a few seconds, so there's this hush between them. "It's a quiet block," he finally begins. "So you'll hear the owls at night."

"Owls?"

He nods. "Barred owls. And … it's a nice walking area around these parts, too." Another pause comes before he fills her in with neighborhood details. "The fire marshal, Bob Hough? He lives across the street, there," Joel says, nodding his head in that direction. "He's married with two little girls. And, well, good folks are on this street. Considerate. Quiet. I actually bought my farmhouse *with* my brother, Brett—before he got married. We roomed together until he got a place of his own. But he stops by and gives me a hand with that," Joel says, pointing to the side yard where his and Faye's properties meet. "I've been finishing up that rock wall there."

"*You* built that wall?"

"I did. It's a work in progress."

Faye stands and takes a few steps in that direction. She squints through the misty evening light, then turns back to Joel. "It's really beautiful. I mean, I've admired it since I moved in."

Joel stands now, too. "It's made with New England fieldstones. Boulders on the bottom. Smaller rocks on top. We've been working on it, on and off, all year."

"So … it's not done?"

"No."

Again she looks over at the stone wall winding down the property. "Looks done to me."

Joel catches up to where she's standing. "It's like the painter's canvas. Always needs something."

"Doesn't that bother you?" she asks, looking up at him now. "To never say it's … complete? A job … well done?"

Joel laughs. "No. It's a tinkering thing for me and my brother. My father, too. He'll bring over stones dug from his garden sometimes."

Faye takes a few steps closer to the wall. "So you never set the paintbrush down," she says over her shoulder.

"It's how you want to look at it." But Joel's not looking at the wall. He's looking at Faye. At her easy smile. At the gold studs glimmering on her ears. "Come on," he says, walking across the yard and motioning for her to follow.

Faye does. Autumn leaves snap beneath their footsteps. Silhouettes of outstretched maple tree branches reach to that dark-blue twilight sky. And the generous light of a low full moon falls on the rock wall, such that the moonlight is almost like soft daylight.

Faye silently meanders along the length of the wall.

And Joel says nothing. He understands what that wall does to people. How it quiets them. Mesmerizes them. Grasses grow among some of the stones; lichen covers others. There's something just … ancient … about the rock and the process itself.

In a moment, beneath the golden moonlight, Faye bends down and slightly moves a stone.

"See?" Joel asks, getting her to look over her shoulder at him standing there. "Never done."

# *nine*

A WEEK LATER, IT'S TIME.

Halloween's come and gone, and November's followed right behind it. The red and yellow foliage has turned brown and fallen from the trees. All along Winter Road, dried leaves swirl in the stiff November breezes. Pumpkins are laced with frost. In the country homes, smoke curls from chimneys.

So early Sunday afternoon, Joel does it. He begins his annual task. It's a long task, too. One that'll take maybe two weeks, start to finish. He's that meticulous with it.

Wearing a brown puffer vest over his flannel shirt, jeans and trail boots, he tugs a wool beanie onto his head and goes outside. And while putting on his gloves, he stands planted at the towering fir tree in his front yard and eyes the width and height of the green boughs.

Then he eyes the plastic tote he'd brought out earlier. It's stuffed with strands of colored lights.

But before he begins stringing them, he fusses with the tree branches. Trims wayward boughs; snaps off dead twigs; climbs the stepladder to prune some of the higher branches. That done, he gets his rake from the shed and cleans up the lawn all around the tree. The sun's shining bright; skies are blue. It's a good day to make a dent in his tree prep.

As he rakes up fir twigs and needles, Faye Weston drives past and pulls into her driveway next door. Joel glances over and when she gets out, he gives a wave—which gets her headed in his direction.

⁓

"Did you hear those *owls* last night? They sounded magnificent!" Faye calls to Joel while veering closer to his yard. "They must've been perched in your tree there." As she says it, she straightens the black cable-knit poncho over her black leggings. And while crossing the lawn, her slouchy boots skim over fallen leaves.

"I did hear them." Joel stops raking and looks her way. "They were really going at it, those night eagles."

"What? I thought you said they were owls."

"Oh, they are," Joel assures her, leaning on his rake as she nears. "But in Native American lore? Owls are sometimes called night eagles."

"I had no idea." Faye brushes a hand over the soft pine needles of Joel's fir tree and looks up at the boughs—trying to spot one of those elusive owls. *"Night eagles."*

"That name was bestowed because of the owls' vision. During the day, *eagles* have superior vision as they soar the skies. Probably the best vision of all the birds."

"But at night?"

"Just the opposite. The eagles' night vision is so weak, they might as well be blind. And in swoops the owl—with the same razor-sharp vision eagles have in the daylight. So there's this whole magical aura of those owls silently flying beneath the pale moonlight and seeing right *into* the darkness—some believe even into our dreams. Giving them what folklore says is the very same power and spirit of the eagles."

"Thus, *night* eagles. What a beautiful story, Joel. One I'm glad to know." When she walks closer, she spots an open tote of colorful lights. "Oh, you light up this grand tree?" she asks then.

"Every year. Strand by strand," he says, motioning up to the top of the tall fir. "Takes a couple of weeks, start to finish."

"Really!" Faye looks at him standing there, leaning on his rake. Dark hair curls out from beneath his wool beanie. A shadow of whiskers covers his jaw.

"My brother's stopping by to help get the top strands on. Then I'll work my way down, a little bit each day."

"Well, I can't *wait* to see it shining in the dark," she tells him, then leans back to take a full gander at the tree. "Must be quite a sight," she adds, right as a car pulls into her driveway.

Joel nods that way. "Company?"

"Oh, that's my dad," she says, venturing back a few steps. "He's helping me swap out some switch plates. So I better get going. But I'll watch out my window for your finished tree," she says with a wave before turning away.

"Say hi to Wayne," Joel calls from behind her. "And enjoy your Sunday."

Faye crosses her leaf-strewn front yard and still thinks of that enchanting night eagle tale. And how the significance and grandeur of the mighty eagle is bestowed upon the wise owls. She looks up at the blue November sky, then glances over her shoulder at Joel—right as he's lifting a strand of lights from that tote.

And catching *her* eye, too.

⌒⌒○

"Lefty loosey, righty tighty," Wayne is saying ten minutes later.

Faye glances at her father opening a small toolbox at the kitchen island. "I know, Dad," she says while unscrewing a tarnished switch plate. "I'm getting very independent."

"And I'm proud of that. But … it worries me sometimes, too."

"What? Why?" She whips around to see her father standing at the refrigerator now. Tapping his own screwdriver in his open hand, he's wearing a crewneck sweater over his flannel shirt and corduroys. He's also looking at her life-list napkin stuck on the fridge door.

"What I mean," he explains, "is that you're getting *too* independent. Like you don't really need *anybody* in your life." With that screwdriver of his, he distinctly taps a certain, particular number on that life list. "*Other* people have great qualities, too."

"*Ach.* Number twenty. Fall in love." Faye resumes her

switch plate lefty-loosey twisting. "Come on, Dad," she says, setting the loosened screw aside. "*Too* independent? When we were in the hardware store buying these new switch plates, I asked *you* to come over and lend a hand." There's silence behind her then—until she looks over her shoulder and meets her father's eye.

"That's not what I'm talking about—and you know it, Faye." He walks to her kitchen table set in a small alcove. A simple chandelier with a lacy drum shade hangs from the ceiling there.

So Faye crosses her arms and waits for him to go on. There are four upholstered chairs at her white-painted, round kitchen table. Each chair is finished with a cream brocade slipcover that ties in a pretty string-bow in the back. Her father pulls out a chair, sits and looks over at her.

"What I'm getting at is … Well," he says, turning up his hands, "you're all settled in at your new job. Any coworkers *there* you're interested in? Someone available to date?"

"Dad! Come on." Faye sighs and resumes her switch-plate work, loosening the last screw in this light-switch plate near the back door. "It's just not like that. And I'm not going to mix business with my personal life, anyway."

"Okay. So what about … Joel?"

"What?"

"Joel. Joel Briggs. I saw you talking in his yard when I drove by. Have you maybe … started seeing him?"

"Oh my gosh, Dad. You are *relentless*, you know that?"

"I just thought …"

Screwdriver still in hand, Faye walks to the table and

70

sits with her father. "Joel's my *neighbor*. We *can't* date. Plus … he's a little older and not *really* my type."

"What do you mean?" Her father stands and looks out a kitchen window—in the direction of Joel's house. "He's a regular hometown guy. Keeps up a nice house. Hosts bingo night. *And* he comes from a good family. Joel's brother is an accountant in town, and I went to high school with their pop."

"Doesn't matter. Not one bit. Because if Joel and I started something up and it *didn't* work out? I'd have to put up a *For Sale* sign here, things would be so weird. And I'm *not* going to even take that chance." Faye stands and now heads over to an electrical outlet mounted in her backsplash. She begins unscrewing its switch plate. "So, no to Joel. Absolutely not." She glances back at her father as he sits again and lines up her new switch plates across the table. "I'm *not* going to ruin a nice friendship. *Or* neighbor, either."

"Sounds like you've given this some thought, Faye."

Faye pauses her switch-plate operation to grab a pen and notepaper. She jots down a few words and sets the paper on the kitchen table.

"What's this?" her father asks.

"*Your* life list, Dad." She gives an affectionate clasp to his shoulder. "Note number one: *No more meddling*."

# *ten*

STEADY. STEADY.

The sound is as steady as a ticking clock. As a heartbeat.

Wednesday morning, it's the only sound Joel hears while running on the paved trail through the woods. There is no wind; the air is cold. And the sound—his sneakered feet pounding the gritty trail—keeps some sort of time. It's regular. And constant.

The soft *thud-thud-thud-thud* of his footsteps keeps even his breathing steady. Coveside Cornucopia's Ye Olde 2K is next week. He wants to shave some seconds off his time this year.

And so he runs in the morning hush.

Around him, leafless tree branches reach far above to the blue November sky. The forest ground is carpeted with twigs and brown leaves. Occasional squirrels rustle through them. And the paved trail winds and weaves through the trees. He's passed few people this morning—

a couple walking; an occasional runner. But the trail's mostly his.

*Thud-thud-thud-thud.*

As he runs, he half unzips his sweatshirt.

*Thud-thud-thud-thud.*

Breathes in ... out.

*Thud-thud-thud-thud.*

It's as peaceful a morning as could be. All is calm. Other than his running, the barren woods are still.

Until suddenly, it feels like the ground is falling.

A thunderous sound comes not from the sky, but from the earth—bringing a sense of movement as well. Joel's step slows as he looks around and peers into the woods. That thudding noise, could it be a large tree falling? He stops, as does another hiker ahead—who spins back around, looking.

In mere seconds, then, a herd of deer comes *crashing* through the trees. There's no cohesiveness to the animals as they run—seemingly out of control. Flashes of tawny brown fly past this way. That way. The thunderous noise Joel's hearing is their panicked hooves hitting the ground. And the sensation of the ground moving comes from the weight of their bodies running chaotically past. They leap; their hooves clatter across the paved trail, then thud onto the solid earth beyond.

And Joel's frozen in place as the deer run past. Just then, two very large deer bolt out of the trees—and straight toward him. Their heavy bodies nearly collide with his as they leap to some escape.

Once the herd disappears far off in the woods, a muffled silence spills in. Joel still stands frozen on the trail. Doesn't move. He can't imagine what spooked the animals, but something surely did as they bolted all around him.

The alarming experience stays with him the rest of the day: as he finally finishes his run; and exclaims to a nearby hiker; and gets home to shower; and even in the tavern that evening.

"Unbelievable, Kevin," Joel says from behind the bar now. He's filling tall glass mugs with warm cider for a special order. But he pauses to shove up his white shirtsleeves. "Those deer scared the *daylights* out of me. They were so panicked, I'm lucky they didn't crash right into me."

"What do you suppose spooked them?" Kevin asks while adding a cinnamon stick to each cider drink.

"No clue. They came out of nowhere. It was really quiet on the trail—then this *thunder* of hooves came crashing by. Thought I was a goner."

"Glad you're okay, Briggs. But man," Kevin says, setting the glass cider mugs on a large tray. "Always expect the unexpected. No?"

Expect the unexpected, all right. Because just then, there she is.

Faye Weston—circa 1600.

It's Addison's historical tour night—which is why Joel's working a late shift. And he nearly sputters when Faye walks in as tour guide, apparently. She wears a brown ankle-length Pilgrim dress with three-quarter sleeves. The soft folds of a long, cream apron drape along the front of the dress; a matching beige ruffle-trimmed shawl is tied over her shoulders. Blonde tendrils of her hair escape from beneath a beige bonnet banded with a wide brown ribbon. She's holding up a battery-operated lantern as several people follow behind her.

"Okay, all," Faye says to the tour group. "Hurry along now."

And they do. Everyone on the tour also holds small lanterns. So the tavern is caught in some time warp as the flickering lights cast a glimmer on the centuries-old wide-planked floor, and the dark paneled walls, and the historical framed paintings there.

"This is Nathaniel Briggs, son of a prominent ship captain," Faye explains moments later, stopping at his portrait. "Back in the 1800s, Nathaniel took over the first tavern in Addison—in the very spot where *this* tavern is now. Some of the architectural features here are actually original, dating back centuries. Including these planked wood floors."

As the group lingers at the framed portraits and seascapes, Joel comes up beside Faye. Quietly, he says near her ear, "Nice threads, Weston."

Faye turns to him and gives a slight curtsy. "I'm tonight's tour guide," she says. "Which was actually number twenty-six on my life list. Join the community." She takes Joel's arm, too, and pulls him aside. *"And when I commit to something,"* she harshly whispers, *"I'm all in."*

Joel eyes her bonnet, her shawl. "I guess so. Where's Lorrie, anyway?" he asks. "She's my regular guide."

"Had a family thing." Faye lifts her illuminated lantern and follows after her group. "I'm covering for her this week," she tells Joel over her shoulder. "Now, folks," she says to her tour then. "Management here is kindly setting out mugs of warm cider for our refreshment. So drink up! We'll be off to view historic New England homes afterward. Saltbox colonials. Ship captains' homes. And Federals that were popular in seaport towns like this one. The Federal rose to prominence in post Revolutionary War times."

And Joel sees—Faye's all in, all right. So he turns back to the bar and sets out the tray of mugs. Cinnamon sticks lean in the warm cider. Caramel squares fill a plate on the tray, too. And in the shadowy tavern, lanterns are raised as the tour group crosses the wooden floors. Just like patrons of yore, they approach the bar for ale and stories before heading out again.

❧

Talk about time travel.

In the span of forty-eight hours, Faye's gone from the seventeenth century to the twenty-first.

From wearing a historical Pilgrim dress and walking cobblestoned paths by lantern light and looking in the tall, narrow windows of a painted Victorian's turret—to this.

To wearing a modern-day deep-gold mockneck sweater with black skinny jeans and Chelsea boots.

To walking into a church hall illuminated with fluorescent ceiling lights and lined with long banquet-style tables. Friday evening, the room is abuzz with chatter and anticipation. Men and women of all ages are settling in, arranging paper bingo games and colorful daubers in front of them. They hang their jackets on chairbacks; they wave to the caller setting up in the front of the room. Wave to Joel. Many stop to chat with him on the way to their tables. The people are all smiles—their eyes twinkling, their faces glowing.

"Welcome one, welcome all—to the grand old bingo hall," Joel announces into his mic. "Good eats in the Grub Room tonight ... It's outtasight. Burgers, hot dogs. There's a grilled ham-and-Swiss-cheese panini special. Chicken Philly with peppers, too."

As his jive talk goes on, Faye notices low cheers and whistles rising from the players.

"Dad," she says to her father when they wait in the Grub Room line for food. "When I said I wanted to do number twenty-one on my life list—try something new? Well, I thought this bingo thing was maybe going to be lame. You know. Sleepy. Kind of ho-hum," she says with a glance through the doorway to where Joel's stationed.

"I told you, Faye." Her father's lifting his tray of food. "Friday nights are hopping here."

Faye orders the ham-and-Swiss panini and follows him to the checkout, then out to the bingo hall.

"Special guest at our table tonight," Wayne says as he sets down his food tray. When he does, his friends Gus, Hank and Pete look his way. "Make room for my daughter."

And as Faye sits with the old-timers eating and doing bingo prep, there are greetings all around. And moving chairs. And a handshake or two.

Then? Then her *Number Twenty-One, Try Something New* ... begins.

A few bingo games are rapidly called. She keeps up with her dauber-dabbing, all while sneaking a bite of that ham-and-cheese panini. Listens to Gus, Hank, Pete and her father compare bingo cards and compete with each other, too. And try to distract one another from winning.

"Okay," Joel announces now. "*This* game is sponsored by Dane's General Store. So the next winner takes home one of their amazing baskets of assorted jams." He holds up a woven basket stuffed with pinecones and faux autumn leaves nestled around locally made jams—raspberry and blackberry; blueberry preserves and apple jelly. "Perfect for that holiday table," Joel goes on. He picks up a leather strap of sleigh bells and gives it a shake. "So get ready to jingle-jam into the next game. It'll be a regular bingo. Starting with … *Ohhh-65,* and a good-luck high five."

Faye does it. She high-fives the guys around her and begins dabbing her dauber. Quickly, a potential bingo takes shape across her card. And … *what?* Is she actually getting … *excited?* She leans toward her father. *"Dad!"* she whispers. *"I might win."* When he glances at her card, she goes on. "Look around to see if anyone else is close."

Wayne does, then discreetly points to Pete.

So Faye hunkers low over her bingo card. And urgently dabs. Dabs once more.

And it happens.

*"Bingo!"* she calls out. Practically jumps up from her seat, too.

When scattered *boos* rise in the room, Joel quiets the crowd. "Hold your cards while we verify."

And he does verify.

And Faye wins.

But when she approaches the front table and Joel

winks at her, then lifts a plush turkey from the prizes, she gets suspicious. Because the Pilgrim frock on that plush turkey oddly resembles the historical Pilgrim attire she donned two nights ago as a tour guide.

"Where's my jam basket?" she asks.

"Oh, my mistake," Joel explains. "That was actually a bigger prize for the Round Robin coming up. *This* was for a regular bingo." He holds out the fluffy turkey-Pilgrim. "Hope you're amenable to it."

Faye just squints at him for a long moment. Joel's dark, wavy hair maybe needs a trim. His unshaven face is scruffy at the end of the day, too. An oversized heathered-cream cardigan is half buttoned over his dark tee and olive jeans. But his eyes? Well, if she's not mistaken, they're *smiling* at hers? With some mischief?

All as he nods for her to take the turkey.

*"Seriously?"* she mutters when he places it in her hands. "In the Grub Room, buster. Right now." *That* she says over her shoulder as she's already headed there.

But there's more, too.

"Arthur," she hears Joel's voice say to someone behind her. "Take over the next game. Got to sit this one out."

⤳◯

Except for two people manning the far checkout table, the Grub Room is empty right now. Joel catches up to Faye at the sandwich station. She's standing there clutching that plush turkey and glaring from the food— to him.

"What?" he asks, turning up his hands.

"What do you mean ... *what?*" She gives that turkey a jiggle. "*This* wasn't my prize—and you know it. This turkey in a *Pilgrim* getup?"

Joel shrugs. "Look familiar?"

"I *knew* it!"

"It's your doppelgänger, Faye. I thought of you the minute it landed on the prize table."

"And *you've* got criminal written all over you." She glances toward the checkout workers. "You swapped prizes and rigged the game!"

"Prove it."

"Come on. You know you did."

Joel gets two sodas and tells her to sit on a chair in the waiting area. He sits beside her and lowers his voice. "Listen. Every now and then, yes, a prize is rigged. Swapped. Whatever."

Faye abruptly stops sipping from her straw. "What?"

He puts up a hand. "Sometimes? As a bingo caller, you just know. Or you see someone really needs a certain item. Or you sense it." He leans low and practically whispers near her ear. "And you bend a rule for the better. A prize gets ... *modified*," he admits, nodding to the turkey.

Faye gives a light laugh. "This is a *church* hall, Joel."

"Right. And the swaps are always with good intentions. And they're rare. And ... And, come on, Weston. Who *else* could win that turkey-Pilgrim?"

"True." She inspects the stuffed animal in her lap. "It does look a little like me on that historical tour."

"I thought so, too." Sitting beside her still, he nudges her arm. "Hope you're not mad."

80

*"I'm not,"* she says with a sigh, then holds the turkey-Pilgrim aloft. "It'll look cute on my kitchen table anyway."

"Well, I'm up. Got to call the next game," Joel says, standing now. "No hard feelings?" he asks while backing toward the door to resume his bingo duty. "Still friends?"

Faye looks long at him. Gives him a small smile and nods, too.

So Joel heads out into the bingo hall. But at the last second, he looks back over his shoulder at Faye Weston.

Faye, who's still smiling as her fingers brush across that plush turkey—right as her eyes glance to him, too.

# *eleven*

FAYE WANTS JUST ONE THING.

Saturday morning, she just wants to stay home.

To stay *inside* her home—especially with that stiff November wind blowing outside.

She wants to stay all cozy in her fleece-lined black leggings and loose turtleneck sweater and fluffy suede-and-shearling ankle boots. But fate's conspiring against her.

Fate, or that cold wind. Because looking out her paned picture window, Faye sees her potted mum toppled beside her lamppost.

So she does it. She decides to dash outside—*quick*—right that plant and hurry back inside to her snug, warm house. After grabbing a Shaker-stitch sweater duster from the coat closet, out she goes. Or trots. Trots straight to the mum. She scoops it up, actually, brings it back to her entry alcove and sits it on the stoop. While she's there, she huddles in her long sweater and adjusts the orange harvest lights she'd strung around her barnboard *Welcome* sign.

And then it happens.

A sudden gust of wind blows.

Blows her front door—shut tight. With a resounding slam, too.

*"Oh, no,"* she whispers, right before turning the knob on that closed front door.

The door that doesn't budge—no matter if she jiggles the knob this way. That way.

No matter if she backs up a step and *glares* at the door—that door that blew shut right behind her.

Now? Now she holds the doorknob and shoves her shoulder against the solidly-in-place wooden door.

And ... nothing.

So she ventures over to her paned front windows. Cupping her hands to the glass, she squints inside. There's her stained-glass teapot lamp on an accent table. She'd turned it on this blustery morning and each stained-glass piece glows pretty. Her cell phone is there, too, charging beside the lamp. She shifts and looks to the side now. There's a straight chair near the front foyer. Her purse is on that chair. And her keys? They're tucked inside that purse.

So Faye returns to the front alcove. She tries the knob— once more—then drops her head and leans against the beautiful, impenetrable, solid wood door that's keeping her from her life inside.

❦

Joel grabs his grocery list off the kitchen counter and gets ready to leave. He scans the list, folds it into his cargo jacket pocket—and stops short when the doorbell rings.

"Faye," he says, opening the door to her standing there on his front porch. She's got on a long sweater over black leggings and shearling-cuffed ankle boots. And in the cold wind, she's holding that rust-colored sweater wrapped tight around her.

"Joel." She gives him a quick smile and brushes aside her wind-tousled hair. "I hope you meant what you said last night at bingo."

"About what?"

"About being friends? Because I really need one right now."

"What's the matter?" he asks, opening the storm door wider and motioning her in.

She stops just inside and tells him an exasperated story about righting a toppled mum when the wind blew her door shut and locked her out.

"*Everything's* inside my house. My keys. My cell phone. But if I can call my father from here, he has a spare house key."

So Joel waits in the kitchen doorway as Faye uses his phone there. He catches pieces of her conversation, too.

"I'll just wait on my stoop for you," she says. A pause, then, "Two hours? Well, I'll be okay. I've got on a heavy sweater, so I won't be too cold."

*"Faye,"* Joel whispers. *"Two hours? Waiting outside?"*

"Hang on, Dad." Faye covers the phone and explains. "My dad brought his dog to the groomer's. Who's actually his sister. It'll be about an hour and a half before he gets back."

"You can wait for him *here*," Joel insists. "Where it's nice and warm."

Faye looks long at him, then nods. "Okay," she says into the phone. "Okay, Dad. I'll actually be waiting next door. At Joel's. See you soon."

When she hangs up, Faye looks a little uncomfortable. She glances around the kitchen, then to Joel. "Oh my gosh," she says then.

"What?"

"Your jacket's on. You were on your way out."

He pulls his list from his coat pocket and flashes it. "Just grocery shopping. But you can stay here. Maybe watch TV."

"No, that's okay." She heads toward his front door. "I don't want to impose. I'll just go back home."

Joel follows behind her. "No way," he says. "I'm not going to let you freeze outside. If you want, just come to SaveRite with me."

"What?" she asks, turning to him.

"Need any groceries?"

"I *do* need a few things, actually," she says with a nod—right before stamping her fluffy booted foot. "*Ach.* I don't have any money on me. And I can't get my purse—which is locked in my house."

"Don't sweat it, Weston." Joel pulls his keys from his jacket pocket and holds open the door. "I'll cover the tab and you can pay me back later."

"Do you work weekends?" Faye asks as they drive down Winter Road.

"Sometimes. But my father's covering for me today."

Joel glances at her in the passenger seat. "He does that. Owned the place for decades and handed the ropes over a few years ago. But he wasn't ready to fully hang up the tavern towel. Not just yet."

"Well that's nice, the way you still work together."

"Yeah. I like having him around there."

They're quiet, then. But Faye can see. Joel's comfortable with her in his pickup truck … talking some. He makes his *living* on easy talk with his patrons. As they drive through the old covered bridge now, the pickup's tires thump over the wood-planked floor.

Joel glances at her again, too. "I can't believe I never saw you this whole past year. That you never came into the tavern. I mean," he says, looking ahead now as they turn onto Brookside Road, "I didn't even think you were from around here."

"Why not?"

"Because *everybody* comes into the tavern—at one point or another."

"It's just that … bars aren't really my scene, that's all."

Joel throws another look her way. "You must have some preconceived notion, Weston. About what the tavern's like. Because it's not really a *bar*, per se. My place isn't like that." He stops at a traffic light. "Joel's Bar and Grille is more a *community* place. Good people are there. Good food." When the light changes, he accelerates and talks more. "And you saw the history inside those walls. The original wood floors. The historic portraits."

"They're striking, I must admit."

Joel nods. "It's a real neighborhood, down-to-earth joint. Good talk. Lots of laughs. Got a great chef, too,

86

changing up the menu. Then we've got line-dancing night on Thursdays. Live music sometimes. Sports. Games."

Faye slightly turns in her seat. The truck's warm, so she loosens her long sweater. Looks over at Joel, too. Sees his dark hair brushing the collar of his cargo jacket. A blue flannel shirt is visible beneath that open jacket. Finally, she somewhat explains herself. "I guess I'm more a coffee shop, bookstore type."

"Got you covered, then. We have a book club that meets once a month." He motions for a car ahead to pull in front of the pickup. "A really lively club, too."

*"Okay."*

He glances at her.

So she turns up her hands. "You're convincing me."

"Good. My tavern's a great spot to hang out. Have dinner, play a trivia game," he says, slowing for a stop sign. "Are you seeing someone? Bring them by."

"Huh. If I were seeing someone, Joel, would I have called my *dad* on the phone?"

"Point taken. So … you're single." Again, he glances at her.

"I am." She looks over at him driving. Looks for a few quiet seconds. "But I'll still give it another go, your bar-and-grille. One of these days," she assures him, right as he turns his pickup truck into the grocery store parking lot.

⁓

SaveRite is busy on a Saturday morning. Joel pushes a shopping cart; Faye hooks a basket on her arm. They start in the produce aisle, where Joel adds tomatoes, salad and some fruit to his cart. When he grabs a rotisserie chicken in the prepared foods, Faye stops him.

"Check the date," she says.

"What? Why?"

"Just check it. They put the newest ones in the back so the *old* ones sell first. But the *new* ones are freshest."

So Joel reaches for a honey-lemon chicken in the back. He lifts the plastic container and compares the date to his first chicken.

*"See?"* Faye whispers, leaning close and pointing to the date. "I told you," she adds when he swaps—yes, he does—his first chicken for the fresh one.

Faye bags a few zucchini now, then moves on.

"I need yellow potatoes," she says, lifting one bag, then another. Carefully, she inspects the potatoes through the clear plastic. She presses them; squints closely.

At the third bag, Joel leans on his cart and just observes.

"What?" Faye asks when she picks up that bag. "What's with the sidelong glance?"

He gives a short laugh. "Faye. Aren't all the potatoes essentially the same?"

"Umm … *no.*" She picks up one of her discarded bags and points to spots on the potatoes. The potatoes in another are monster sized, which she promptly informs him will be *so* dry. "I work hard and pay good money for this food. So I want the best value—*and* quality."

Once the yellow potatoes are thoughtfully chosen, they make their way to the meat case—where Faye rings for the butcher.

"After you," Joel says, motioning to her when the butcher approaches.

She looks at Joel, gives a quick nod, then turns. The butcher's standing on the other side of the meat case and wiping a hand on his white apron.

And already Joel's smiling. Because he knows *just* what's coming.

"I'd like exactly one-and-a-half pounds of ground beef," Faye informs the butcher.

"Have you checked our pre-wrapped packages in the case there? I'm sure you'll find something close," the butcher suggests.

"No." Faye shakes her head. "It has to be *exactly* one-and-a-half pounds. One-point-five pounds. And I'd like your *eighty*-percent ground beef."

"We have a special on the ninety-percent lean," the butcher advises her. "You don't want that?"

*Oh,* Joel thinks with a wry smile. *Wrong question, guy.* He also watches Faye step closer to the case.

"No. I need your *eighty* percent. It's the sweet spot for my meatloaf." When the butcher nods and starts to prepare her order, she goes on   stopping him in place. "It's just that the eighty percent has the right amount of fat to enhance the flavor. That smidge more of fat *also* keeps the meat moist, so it doesn't dry out while cooking."

"Of course." The butcher then prepares her *exact* one-and-one-half-pound ground beef order.

"Thank you," Faye says. She takes the wrapped meat, tucks her blunt-cut hair behind an ear and carefully sets the ground beef beside the potatoes and zucchini in her basket.

She and Joel walk up and down the remaining aisles of SaveRite—snacks, and paper goods, and bread. As Joel shops, and drops paper towels and a loaf of whole-grain bread and a bag of chips into his cart, he's amused—and a little dumbfounded—while listening to Faye's matter-of-fact, soft voice. She's been distractedly explaining how the perfect meatloaf is all about timing.

"Potatoes and zucchini in at one time. Meat at *exactly* fifteen minutes later."

"Exactly?"

"*Precisely.* Because those veggies have to come in and out of the oven to be turned and drizzled with oil. And it's all synchronized with the meat timing. Because if the meatloaf cooks for even *one minute* longer than it should, it dries out. Right away. That's why I need an exact amount of meat. To coordinate with my timing."

They finish up in the dairy row. Joel adds some butter, and yogurt, and creamer to his cart.

"I have it down to a science, Joel," she says as they turn into a checkout line. "And it works."

Out at his pickup, they load in the groceries—his in the bed, hers in the cab with them—and drive back to Winter Road. Right when Joel is dropping Faye off at the curb, he waves to her father pulling his car in the driveway.

"Wait," Joel says to Faye before she leaves. He reaches over and grabs a pen from the glove box, then scrawls his cell phone number on her brown-paper shopping bag. "It's good to have a neighbor's number," he's saying while writing. "For emergencies like today. So give me yours, too." When she does, he adds it to his cell phone contacts.

Finally, Faye takes her neatly packed bag and gets out. She walks around the truck and taps on his window, too—so he opens it.

"Wait here," she tells him. "I'll get your money inside. For the food." As she says it, she hefts up her grocery bag.

"No. No, Faye." He puts his truck in gear. "There's no need to pay me."

"What?" she asks, backing up a few steps when his truck starts moving.

He looks out at her. That November wind is still going, and wisps of her hair blow across her face. "Just save me a hunk of that meatloaf, okay?" he asks, nodding to her bag. "And we'll call it even."

Joel drives back toward his house, then. As he does, he glances at Faye's reflection in his rearview mirror. Brushing aside her windblown hair, she's still watching him from the curb—brown leaves swirling at her booted feet.

# twelve

THAT EVENING, JOEL QUIETLY ARRANGES one plate, one napkin, one glass on his kitchen table. He adds a fork and knife, too. Moves the salt and pepper shakers closer to his dish. Gets the butter from the refrigerator. And lastly, sets down a folded newspaper section. Behind him, a pot of green beans heats on the stove; a hefty potato bakes in the oven.

Finally, he gets that fresh rotisserie chicken from the fridge. After stringing more light strands around his big fir tree all afternoon, he's got an appetite. Could eat that whole bird, actually. But he'll save a few slices for a chicken-sandwich snack later on. For now, he puts the chicken on a plate and lifts a carving knife from the drawer—right as his cell phone dings. So he grabs it off the kitchen counter and reads the text message. It's from Faye.

*Dinner for your troubles?*

He smiles, then thumb-types his answer. *When?*

*Now!* is her prompt response. *Meatloaf just came out of oven. Setting on stovetop for 20 minutes. Can you be here by then?*

Joel just nods. Nods, types back *On my way*, then turns off the stove burner and dumps the canned beans. Shoves that rotisserie chicken in the refrigerator. The baked potato, too. Heads straight to the coat closet—and stops. Looks down at his blue plaid flannel loose over navy thermal tee. Looks at his coats, too, and grabs the corduroy-trimmed canvas vest. Stopping in front of a wall mirror near the door, he adjusts the vest collar, runs his fingers through his needs-a-trim hair and away he goes.

It's cold outdoors, the November wind still blustering. So after moving aside the large tote of tree lights on his porch, he snaps that vest closed. Hurrying down the steps then, he shoves his hands in his vest pockets and trots across the lawn to Faye's bungalow. In the early evening shadows, its peaked roofline is a silhouette against the dark lavender sky. But the house's paned windows are golden with lamplight. And the entry alcove is illuminated by tiny orange lights strung around his barnboard *Welcome* sign leaning near the door.

Joel stops there, hesitates, then rings the bell.

⌒⌒◯

"Oh my God." Sitting at Faye's kitchen table later, Joel says this around a mouthful of food. "Your meatloaf is out of this *world*, Weston."

Faye, sitting across from him at a white-painted round table, simply gives a haughty shrug. Oh, there might be a twinkle in those hazel eyes of hers, too—it's hard to tell with the way her long bangs sweep across them. But they sit there and just eat in her cozy kitchen nook. A drum-shade chandelier glows above them. Their forks and knives click on the plates. Wineglasses sparkle. The room is warm. Joel shoves up his thermal shirtsleeves and glances around. A white chair rail runs the length of the pale gray walls. And beside the table, a large mirror resembling a paned window leans on the mantel over a small fireplace. The mirror's frame is dark gray; a simple glass vase of errant green sprigs sits in front of it.

And their talk is light and easy.

But mostly, they eat. Because, yes, Faye does have her meatloaf recipe down to a science. The roasted sliced potatoes and zucchini, too. All of it is like, well, magic. Meatloaf gets dragged through steak sauce. Ketchup. Baked wedges of yellow potatoes are forked and dabbed through juices on the plate. It's the kind of meal that you have to force yourself to push back from, but then find your fork picking at more.

Afterward, Joel rinses off his plate and silverware at the sink and loads everything into the dishwasher. There's a small TV mounted beneath Faye's painted kitchen cabinets. When she switches it on to the local news, a meteorologist is giving the forecast.

"Sunny tomorrow," Joel notes, watching the weather map. "I can get more lights strung on my tree."

Faye, meanwhile, brings a few more things to the sink area. A spatula. Ketchup bottle. Her own plate—which she's still stabbing her fork at to get every last morsel of meatloaf and veggies. News anchors report the headlines while he and Faye keep wiping and clearing. Leftovers get put on clean plates, wrapped and refrigerated. Oven pans get scoured and rinsed. When the news is over, Faye switches the TV channel. She stops on an old Christmas movie just beginning.

"Oh, this is one of my favorites," she says, slowly sitting on a breakfast-island stool and watching the opening credits. The camera pans an old-fashioned, bustling downtown. Shoppers bundled in coats and hats hurry along sidewalks dusted with snow. Bells toll. Swags of balsam garland loop over paned shop windows.

"What movie is it?"

"*The Gathering*. Takes place in a beautiful old New England town," she says, nodding to the TV. "And in a gorgeous colonial home there."

"I've never seen it," Joel tells her as he closes the dishwasher.

"*Really?* Well, grab a stool."

He joins her, then, at the island. Together they watch the opening scenes. Neither one talks as the movie begins. As the main character, Adam, walks with his doctor along those downtown streets. The two men pause on a bridge over a wide stream fed by a waterfall. It's here that Adam learns how much time he has left to live.

"*I'll be right back,*" Faye whispers, then hurries out of the kitchen.

But Joel stays put. He watches this Adam come to grips with his grim news at Christmastime. After a few moments, though, Joel feels a little awkward being here like this. So as a pensive flute whispers from the TV, he stands and shoves down his shirtsleeves. "I don't want to overstay my welcome. Think I'll take off now," he calls out in Faye's direction—down some dark hallway. "Let you enjoy your movie," he goes on, lifting his canvas vest off a chairback. "You know, I was only supposed to have a slab of meatloaf," he vaguely says, slipping on his vest while watching this Adam's bleak realization settle.

"What?" Faye's voice calls back from that hallway. "Just stay, I don't care," she says, hurrying into the kitchen nook. She sits at the table there, leans over and pulls tall, thick slipper socks on over her black leggings. Looks over at him, too. "Don't you like the movie?"

"I do." Joel turns to her as he's snapping his vest, then looks over his shoulder as this Adam's getting in touch with his estranged wife. "I'm glued to it, actually."

Faye stands. "Listen. You're just going to go home and watch the rest there, anyway. So come on," she says, motioning to her family room. "We'll watch it here. *And*," she adds, her voice lifting with temptation, "I have some dark-chocolate, sea-salted peanut butter cups for dessert."

"Let me guess. They're the best?" Joel asks.

When Faye only silently nods, he just stands there in her kitchen. The movie plays behind him as he watches Faye watching him from beneath those blonde bangs. A soft knit scarf is looped over her long sweater. They're quiet, with only Adam talking to his wife on the TV screen.

All it takes to change Joel's mind about staying is Faye turning up her hands in question. Then? Well, he rehangs his vest on the chair, switches off the kitchen TV and settles with her in the family room. The paneled walls there are painted pale gray. A large-screen TV stands atop a shelved entertainment console between two paned windows. Faye gets the movie on, dims a pedestal table lamp and sets the TV remote on a planked coffee table. Only then does she curl up among throw pillows on a heathered-gray sofa while motioning for Joel to sit, too. He'd been standing in the doorway and walks now to a tufted-back easy chair beside the couch.

They're quiet again, drawn into the film's drama unfolding before them.

Riveted to one last family reunion being planned.

Glued to a nostalgic attic scene where old toys and decorations are lifted and revived.

"Why Mr. Briggs," Faye's soft voice comes during a touching scene in the family's old colonial home. "Is that a tear in your eye I see?"

"What?' Joel sits up in that upholstered chair. He blinks a few times, too. Maybe there might have been a *glisten* of emotion there.

"Don't cry now," Faye lightly warns, shaking a finger. "You'll be doomed to a season of Christmas sadness. So ... hold those tears."

He looks at her, waves her off and resettles back in that easy chair.

Together, they watch the good, old-fashioned Christmas tale. And when a commercial comes on, Faye gets up from her sofa-lounging.

"I'll go get those peanut butter cups. But first ..."

He watches as she stands there in her sweater and leggings and slipper socks. The room is shadowy. A stained-glass teapot lamp glimmers on a window table. With amusement, he waits. She's contemplating *something* while she stands there, half turned away but still watching him, too.

"Do you like your peanut butter cups chilled in the fridge?" she asks then, heading toward the kitchen now. "Or at room temp?" her voice calls back.

# *thirteen*

IF FAYE WESTON'S GOTTEN GOOD at anything, it's doing two things at once.

Like right now, late Wednesday morning. While sitting at her desk at work, she's checking the time all as her eyes skim the draft of Silver Settings' company newsletter on her computer screen.

*"Suitable to every home,"* she whispers while reading about the *Flatware of the Month—Classic Homestead.* She keeps going, first approving the sweet potato casserole Thanksgiving recipe. Next up? The color photo of a country-style Thanksgiving-set table with Silver Settings' flatware glimmering at every place setting. Finally, a *Clearance Special* for their customers. The discontinued, very basic *Farmstead* style should sell well during the holiday season.

So again, Faye does two things at once.

She hits the *Send* button—delivering the newsletter to thousands of customers, all while standing to lift her black bomber jacket off the coatrack. Slipping the jacket on over her long beige sweater dress and black Chelsea boots, she grabs her purse and rushes out the door.

Yes, to do two things at once—shopping during her lunch hour.

Which is why, ten minutes later, she's with her friend Sadie at Lighting Lodge. They wander through the carriage house where the shop's located. Above them, crystal chandeliers sparkle. There are diamond crystals and teardrop crystals. Icicles and pendalogues. She and Sadie move into the showroom off the lobby to find table lamps with black shades and candelabra wall sconces and vintage floor lamps of bronze and cherry wood. Polished brass glimmers; lights shine all around.

All the while, Sadie's telling Faye about her latest offering as the town of Addison's event planner.

"It's called Merry Match and supports small businesses. So far, I've secured Whole Latte Life, Dane's General Store, the dance studio, Joel's Bar and Grille, Luigi's Pizza. Each participating business will have a candy-cane heart displayed in a front window. *Any* customer can then ask for the Merry Match special."

"Wait." Faye looks up from a ceramic lamp she's holding. "Are you telling me that Merry Match is really a … dating service?"

"Well, yes. But done Addison's way. Even Cooper Hardware's participating. Because, I mean, you can have a sleigh-ride date. Or heck, fall in love by their popcorn machine!"

"You know … not every holiday love story ends up like yours and Harry's."

"We'll see." Sadie touches a brocade lampshade. "Anyway, Merry Match is a win-win for *everyone*. It'll drive business to local shops during the holidays. And maybe some love matches will get made, too?" She squints at Faye then.

"Why are you looking at me like that?" Faye suspiciously asks.

"Oh my gosh, Faye! Can I add *you* to the Merry Match date list?"

"Sadie!" Faye leans over and peeks into the furniture showroom. "I'm looking for a piece of furniture—not a guy. And *you* obviously had an ulterior motive when you *agreed* to my shopping lunch."

"Maybe." Sadie picks up a painted bedside lamp. "But it'd be for *your* benefit, too."

"How? With blind dates?"

Sadie sets down that lamp and looks over at Faye. "Think of number twenty on your life list. Fall in love?"

"That was never *my* number. My father added it."

"And *you* never crossed it off, I noticed."

"I know." Faye smiles with a small shrug. "But I'm good with things, Sadie. I'm happy," she says, pulling the on/off chain on a floor lamp. "I have a great job I go to every day. And a beautiful new house. I'm taking classes. And I'm independent." Faye wanders to the doorway of the shop's furniture showroom again. "Actually," she says over her shoulder, "I've never been better."

Sadie catches up to her and clasps her arm. "You still can't give up on number twenty. Especially this time of year. Because you're right, I *do* have a beautiful Christmas love story with Harry. So I want other people," she says, "you included, to have that possibility. There's nothing sweeter than falling in love at Christmastime. So at least *think* about joining Merry Match?"

Faye takes a long breath. "I'll get back to you, Sadie. Because *this*," she insists, tugging Sadie with her into the furniture room, "is the *only* decision I'm making today."

⁓

A steady stream of customers is in and out of the tavern. Some of them chat with Joel as he's tinkering in the open entranceway. He talks, all while tightening the decorative hinge plates on his vintage black-painted entrance door.

> From one arriving patron: *Cleaned out the linen closet*, he says, handing Joel a large bag. *Donating this brand-new fleece blanket to your New Year's Sweep Night.*
> From Joel: *Thanks, guy. Can never have enough blankets for the outdoor-table crowd.*
> Another patron, this one an older woman: *Your parents still making all the whisk brooms, Joel?*
> Joel's answer: *Oh, yeah. Mom and Dad are at it overtime now.* He points with the screwdriver to an open carton just inside the tavern. It's brimming with ribbon-and-twine-bedecked mini corn brooms.
> From a man leaving: *Getting ready to sweep out this year and welcome in the new?*
> Joel: *That's the idea.*

"Hey, Joel," the next patron says.

Joel straightens to see Faye walking closer. She's got

on a black leather bomber over a long sweater dress, tights and black ankle boots. Her shoulder-length blonde hair is down today; silver studs glimmer on her ears. "Well, my friend," Joel tells her. "Good to see you."

She gives him an easy smile. "Told you I'd give your place another try. I need a quick lunch to go today. Thought I'd grab it here?"

"Excellent." Joel shoves that screwdriver in his back pocket and closes the door behind him. "Come on," he says, motioning Faye to the bar. "What can I get you?"

Faye sits right at the Trouble Tree. And after Joel puts in her order for an overstuffed chicken wrap with blue cheese dressing, baked chips and a pickle, they talk some.

"Your tree here's filling up," Faye says as she lifts an acorn ornament from the bowl. "What's most on people's minds?"

"Runs the gamut. You know, anything from relationships," Joel explains, cuffing back his white shirtsleeves, "to Christmas shopping troubles."

"Christmas shopping?"

"Sure. Like ... what to get for Aunt Mabel." Joel draws a draft beer for a waitress, then turns back to Faye. "Some troubles involve health issues. Others are simple indecision, like should I get a fresh-cut tree or fake."

"Oh." Faye says no more as she fiddles with that acorn. Her eyes stay steady on that tree, too. And thoughts stream through her mind.

Particularly thoughts of Sadie's Merry Match event.

Because sometimes, well, maybe love *does* need a little nudge.

But still, Faye typically doesn't do that kind of thing—blind dating.

Though Sadie's way of doing it *could* be fun.

"Got a trouble today, Faye?" Joel asks, leaning on the bar. "Some leftover New Year's tears you're holding back?"

"No, nothing like that." Faye looks from the tree to Joel. Oh, how she'd love to run the whole Merry Match thing by him—he's a hosting business after all. But she feels awkward, him being a new friend and such. *Aargh*, what to do? She gives Joel a quick smile. "Do you know Sadie Welles?" she finally asks.

"Yeah, Harry's girl. I'm friends with Harry."

Again, Faye hesitates. And squints through the tavern shadows at Joel. Behind her, the lunch crowd talks; dishes and forks clatter; waitresses breeze by. "Well," Faye goes on. "I did some shopping on my lunch break. With Sadie, I mean. And here's my dilemma." Faye pauses while ceremoniously hanging her trouble acorn on the tree. "We were at Lighting Lodge. In the old home of your ancestor, right? Captain Josiah?"

"You got it," Joel says, crossing his arms in front of him. "In that big stone house on the hill."

"Yes, a beautiful place. And there were some refurbished furniture pieces in the shop, too … so I'm back and forth between two end tables," she admits—rather than admit her latest dilemma about joining Merry Match. "Black distressed or gray. Both tables have a skeleton-key drawer pull. And both are on hold for me. I have to make a decision in an hour."

Joel squints at her from behind the bar. "This is a trouble?"

"Um … yes. It's on my life list. Number thirty: Commit to a home décor style. My apartment furniture was a hodgepodge of things. College finds. Tag-sale items. So, yes." Faye touches the acorn she just hung. "It's a trouble. I want my new house to be more … defined." She looks up at Joel now. Sees scruffy whiskers on his face. Sees his dark eyes watching her as he stands there in his work outfit: black vest over white button-down and black pants. And she shrugs. "Am I modern farmhouse style? Country chic?" She motions around the historic tavern. "Traditional?"

"Well, Miss Weston. In your own inimitable way, I'm sure you'll precisely come to the right conclusion," Joel says as the waitress delivers her packaged lunch. "And when you do," he adds as Faye stands to leave, "you're welcome to remove your trouble acorn from the tree."

❧

Early that evening, Joel's finishing up some paperwork in the tavern office. As he opens his desk drawer, his cell phone dings with a message. It's Faye.

*Number 30—done,* she texts him. She immediately sends along a photograph of her new end table with her stained-glass teapot lamp on it. So she went with the gray.

*My design style,* she goes on with her texting. *Welcome to … Hipstoric.*

*What?* Joel thumb-types back. *Is that a typo?*

No surprise that his cell phone *immediately* rings. And

when he answers it, Faye just starts talking before he can get a word in.

"Hipstoric," she's saying. "Doesn't it have a great ring to it? It's so me."

"What the heck is hipstoric?"

"The latest design trend. It's actually a combination of two words—hip and historic. You know, old fused with new. Like my fresh, *new* gray table with the *old* skeleton-key drawer pull. It's all about the mix."

As she goes on, Joel simply listens. Leans back in his chair, lifts his feet up onto his desk and listens to Faye's voice talk about bringing a personal touch blended with nostalgia to her little country bungalow. And how hipstoric is good for the environment, too, keeping old furniture out of the landfills. And that she's starting small, being *very* thoughtful of what pieces she'll select.

"It's all about character," she's saying now, her voice soft yet insistent in his ear. "And being in tune with the vibe of a home."

*⁓*

"Snow, snow, snow?" meteorologist Leo Sterling asks during the news later that night.

Joel's home now and having a sandwich in his living room. He leans over the coffee table and watches Leo on the TV.

"No, no, no," the meteorologist declares. "This weekend's Ye Olde 2K is looking to be a-okay, folks! Chilly, but no snow anywhere in sight—so running conditions will be just right."

*Good,* Joel thinks when he clears his plate and tosses out his napkin. It's garbage night, too, so he ties up his kitchen bag and brings it out to his trash can—which he then rolls down to the curb. On the way, he passes the big fir tree in his yard. It's just about all strung with lights— but not lit up yet. After his father and brother help give a final adjustment to the top strands and star, the tree will be ready.

In the dark of night, Joel walks back up the driveway to his farmhouse. Golden lamplight fills the windows. Wall lanterns cast a glow beneath the front-porch overhang. Next door, though, Faye's house is dark at this late hour. It's a work night; she must've turned in already. Her bungalow is just a shadow against the black sky.

But the owls are up. Up and hooting.

*Who-who. Who-whooo,* Joel hears, over and over. One barred owl, then another, talk in the night. Their calls are throaty and ancient sounding. He stops on the porch and leans against a post. The cold air is still. The only sound comes from those owls. They keep at it. *Who-who. Who-whooo.* One is near; one muted in the distance.

Leaning on the porch post, Joel looks to the sky for any motion.

For even the *possibility* of feathered wings outstretched.

Of the night eagles swooping through the darkness.

# *fourteen*

SATURDAY MORNING, ADDISON COVE GLISTENS beneath a November-blue sky.

Faye approaches the cove and sees it all—the water, and the nearby tents selling patchwork quilts and sweatshirts and crafts. There are food trucks, too, with people already lined up at them. Coveside Cornucopia is in full swing.

But it's the cove that Faye takes in. Hundreds of years ago, this very spot was a shipping port for sea trade from the West Indies and British colonies. She can imagine the local ships with billowing sails returning home. The ship captains disembarking; their wives watching from widows' walks on nearby prominent colonials.

Today, though? Runners stream into the cove parking lot. Faye is one of them, a straggler at the end. Running Ye Olde 2K was more a sightseeing journey through Addison's historic neighborhoods than anything else. She crosses the finish line now and heads to a refreshment tent with the others.

"Faye," a voice calls right as she's guzzling from a water bottle. She turns to see Joel standing there. He's got on a long-sleeve tee over jogger pants and sneakers. The tee's sleeves are shoved up; he holds a bottle of water, too—which he's pressing to the side of his perspiring face.

"Joel," she says, walking over. "Thought I saw you before."

"Yeah." He takes a swig of that water. "Tried to beat my old time."

"Did you?"

"By a few seconds."

Faye nods and looks to another guy standing there, too.

"Oh, hey," Joel says, turning to him. "This is my brother, Brett. We ran the race together."

"Brett who is booking," Brett tells her when he shakes her hand. "Nice to meet you, Faye. I've heard your Joel's neighbor?" he asks while backing away.

"I am."

"And I'm *really* sorry. But my wife's setting up her food tent, over yonder," he says, hitching his head toward the cove. "I've got to get there and take our daughter off her hands."

When Faye waves goodbye, Joel walks closer. "So you made it to the finish line," he says.

"Slow and steady may not *win* the race, but it finishes it," Faye tells him, then takes another drink from her water bottle. "So," she continues, "number eighteen on my life list? Run a marathon?"

"Seriously?" Joel interrupts.

Faye nods as, still a little winded, they walk side by side to cool off. "Ye Olde 2K will suffice. Number eighteen—run. *Done.*"

"Kudos." Joel tips his water bottle to hers in a toast.

They slowly keep walking. Their sneakers tread across the dirt-and-stone parking area. Faye fans her gray fleece vest over black leggings. "Not to mention," she continues, dabbing a bead of perspiration from her face, "number *nineteen*—buy a house—also done." She looks past the lingering runners then.

"Waiting for someone?" Joel asks.

"My father. He said he'd meet me here after my run."

Joel looks over, then back to her as he slows his step. "So eighteen and nineteen are checked off your life list. Thirty-five things by thirty-five, right?"

Faye toys with her water bottle cap. "You got it. And just like this race, slowly but surely I'm getting there."

"But last New Year's Eve, you mentioned a troublesome nineteen *and* twenty on your list." He squints at her now. "What's the elusive number twenty?"

"*Ach*, number twenty! I don't want to talk about that one."

"But we're friends," Joel insists. "And friends tell each other this kind of thing."

"Not this, they don't."

"Come on, how bad can it be?"

"No, no, no."

They still slowly walk and sip. People mill around them. Further away, the Plymouth Dock event is going on at the banks of the cove. A boat there is rigged with billowing white sails; children are dressed in Pilgrim costumes as they replicate early settlers arriving in New England.

But Joel's stuck on her number twenty.

"Let me guess. Number twenty. *Hm.* Learn to yodel?"

Faye lightly hits him.

"Write a novel?"

"No."

"Tell a dirty joke?"

"No!" Faye laughs. "*Ugh*, number twenty wasn't even my idea. My *father* wrote it on the list."

"Okay. I'm waiting …"

Faye briefly covers her face with her hand. "Fall in love," she admits then.

"Huh," Joel says with some amusement. "Love. That's a tough one, Weston. There's no one-stop shop for it."

"No kidding." Faye tips up her bottle and finishes her water. Glances around the crowd for her father, too. "And my friend Sadie? She *really* got hung up on that one on my list—so she roped me into this Merry Match thing she's putting on for the town."

"Ah. You didn't mention that before."

"Because it's … matchmaking! And *completely* embarrassing."

"Not really." Joel takes Faye's empty bottle and drops hers and his into a recycle bin. "Sadie's probably a good matchmaker. Because … well, look at her and Harry. Two years strong now." Joel runs a hand back through his damp hair. "I even signed up the tavern as a hosting spot."

"Sadie mentioned that."

"And it's all in good fun. So you let me know how it goes, Weston."

Faye gives his shoulder a nudge. "You're not seeing

anyone, Joel. *You* could sign up too, you know."

"Hell no." Joel backs up a step. "I'll leave the horror stories to you. And hey, if you want to share them, there's a stool with your name on it at the Trouble Tree."

"Ha! So you *don't* think this can work."

"I hope you'll prove me wrong."

"I'll try." Faye looks past him now. "Oh, there's my dad with his dog. Roxy," she says. "Up ahead there." She starts jogging in that direction. And when she looks back over her shoulder at Joel, he's giving a wave to her father, then to her, too.

⁂

It doesn't take long.

By midafternoon, Joel trades his tee and joggers and sneakers for jeans and a flannel and beanie and a puffy vest. Gloves, too. Gray clouds have rolled in on a cold November wind.

That's not all that's happened.

His aluminum ladder is fully extended and leaning against the tall fir tree in his front yard. And Joel's standing at the top of that ladder. He glances down below to where his father and brother both hold the ladder steady for him.

And he gets the job done.

He secures the star on top of his tree.

When he gives a thumbs-up to the others, they give a *Woot!* and a whistle back before Joel carefully descends that ladder. His booted feet thud on each rung until he's finally back on the frozen ground.

Now the tree just needs its finishing touches. The three of them tuck lights here, and adjust boughs there, and secure light strands with tree clips. While they fuss, they argue, too, about which farm stand has the best pumpkin pie for their Thanksgiving dinner. *Don't go here, try there. They had nicer pumpkins, so their pies will be good.*

The argument is interrupted with Brett pointing out some bare spots on the tree branches, and with their father switching on the tree lights so they can better gauge the illumination.

But before long, they get back to the talk at hand. Brett mentions going for his final tux fitting for Derek and Vera's wedding.

"You and Mom babysitting Harriet that night, Dad?" Joel asks, clipping a light strand to the tree.

"Sure are. And what about you?" his father asks back.

"What about me?"

"You bringing someone to that swanky affair?"

"No." Joel looks over at him. His father has a wool cap pulled on. A scarf is wrapped around his plaid jacket collar, too. "Going stag."

"Come on, Joel." His father walks closer. "You're what? Thirty-eight already? We should be getting ready for *your* wedding."

"What do you want me to do about it, Dad?"

"Well. What about that Denise?" his father persists. "You had a good thing going with her for a while."

"Water under the bridge. Didn't work out for us." Joel heads to the porch and puts the tree-clip package into his plastic tote now. "Anyway, I haven't talked to Denise in ages," he calls back. "Last I heard? She was in upstate New York."

113

"What about your neighbor?" Brett asks as he closes up the ladder.

"What about her?"

"Ask *her* as your guest," Brett tells him.

"No." Joel snaps the tote shut tight. "We're just friends, guy."

His father turns to him on the porch now. "Who are we talking about, Joel?"

"His neighbor. Faye," Brett lets on as he stands there holding the closed-up ladder. "I met her this morning at the 2K. Really nice lady."

"Oh. A single girl?" his father asks Joel.

Joel hefts up that tote and heads toward the garage. "Single, beautiful, smart, confident—and my *neighbor!* And *that's* an issue, Dad. So it's not like that. You know, with the dating stuff."

"Why not, son?" his father calls after him.

"Could be worse ways to meet," Brett adds as he lugs that ladder behind Joel to the garage.

"Keep it down, you two, would you? See what I mean?" Joel asks when they pile into his garage. "I don't need all of Winter Road hearing this. Knowing my personal business. And," he says, all while thinking of his Merry Match talk with Faye that morning, "she's starting up with someone, anyway."

So that's that. Case closed for his brother and father.

But not for Joel.

Because why else does a curious interest in Faye stay on his mind the rest of the day? He thinks about her when he drives to work. And while having dinner in his office at the tavern. And when he relieves Kevin tending bar.

114

And what it all comes down to is one—just one—question.

A question that presents one new *trouble* in his life.

So ... he does it. While working the bar, Joel secretly lifts an acorn ornament from the bowl of them there. He discreetly hangs that acorn, too, off to the side on the Trouble Tree. As he does, he contemplates his new, nagging trouble.

Would Faye Weston have been the one—if she didn't live right next door?

# *fifteen*

As soon as Joel's coffeepot is percolating Sunday morning, it's on again with his puffy vest, beanie and gloves. Out with the stepladder, too, once he's in the yard. After all, it's the Sunday before Thanksgiving.

The Sunday before he lights up his towering fir tree.

The countdown has begun.

So after picking up a telescoping pole, he climbs a few ladder rungs, hooks some loose light strands and tucks them into the boughs. Gets them ... okay, *just so*. A few strands moved here, reposition the ladder, a few there.

But ... wait.

From standing three rungs up on the ladder, Joel can see the little neighborhood green down the street. It's just a patch of tended lawn off the side of the road. Some tall trees grow there, too. And wrapped *around* one of the trees? There's a tree bench—a wooden seat encircling the entire, wide tree trunk. The bench is painted green and has a slatted back to lean against. Occasionally, a neighbor or two sits there soaking in the peaceful spot.

Today, it's Faye.

Joel spots her from his vantage point. So he looks from there to his fir tree, then climbs down the ladder. And hesitates. But then he goes inside and pours fresh coffee into two take-out cups before walking outside again.

⌒∾◯

While bent over her papers, Faye feels a tap on her shoulder. She looks up to see Joel standing there. He's got on a down vest over a flannel shirt, jeans and work boots. A wool cap is pulled over his dark hair.

"Coffee?" he asks, his gloved hands holding two cups.

"Oh, perfect. But how—" She looks from him, back down the street.

"I was fussing with my tree lights and spotted you from my ladder."

"Fussing? Still the artist who can't put down his paintbrush?"

"Must be my thing," Joel says, lowering a coffee.

She takes the cup and sips from it. "Hits the spot. It's a cold morning."

"It is," Joel agrees, still standing there. "So what brings you out from your nice, warm home?"

"A change of scenery, I guess." Faye lifts the papers in her lap. "Thought it might help me answer this questionnaire."

"For what? A new job?"

"No, I love Silver Settings. This is actually … okay, it's my Merry Match paperwork. Sadie needs some details to arrange the fix-ups."

"Details? Like what?"

"Oh … personal qualities and preferences. Which businesses I'd prefer hosting my dates."

"Really." Joel shifts his stance and glances down at the questionnaire. "You don't have to do all that, Faye."

"I don't?"

Joel looks at her for a long second. "I'm right here," he tosses out.

"Ha! Thanks for trying to save me the pain of not one, but *several*, blind dates." She looks from her papers to him. "I appreciate it, my friend. But," she goes on with a firm nod. "I signed on with Sadie and … I'm committed."

"Okay. So how does this all work?"

"Well, Sadie will review the questionnaires, then match the candidates up so the dates will hopefully be compatible. I guess all I'll get then is my date's first name. No personal contact is exchanged. No last names. Not even phone numbers. Everything is arranged by Sadie and her staff. Except for the location—which I get to pick. You know, so that we're … *comfortable*."

Joel nods, then sips his coffee. "Sadie dropped off candy-cane hearts at the tavern last week. I guess me or Kevin will set them on the date tables?"

"Yes! When we arrive, we're supposed to let our hosts know. But Sadie coordinates the day and time for the participants. And we awkwardly show up and take it from there." Faye sets down her coffee and lifts her papers and pen now. "Which is why I need to *carefully* answer these questions—so Sadie can start making the connections."

"So this whole Merry Match thing hinges on the questionnaire."

"Which requires more *introspection* than I'd thought."

Joel sits beside her on the tree bench, then. "Maybe I can help with the questions. Try me." Holding his coffee cup, he leans forward, elbows on his knees, and looks back at her sitting there. "Let's find your Mr. Right."

"Oh my God." Faye squints at him. "Are you for real?"

"Of course." His eyes watch hers; his expression is serious. "Fire away, Weston."

❧

Joel looks back at Faye. She's wearing her honey-gold plaid jacket over a thick sweater, jeans and ankle boots. Fingerless gloves are on her hands; her hair is down; her eyes, locked onto his. And he waits for her first question.

"Okay," she finally says, glancing at that questionnaire. "First up? Yes-or-no questions."

Joel sips his coffee and nods.

Faye clears her throat. "Do you set life goals and focus on achieving them?"

"Oh, yes," Joel answers. "Check *and* check. You might want to bold and *underline* your answer on that one."

Faye nudges him, checks *Yes* and continues. "Next. Are you very selective about who you'll date?"

Joel raises an eyebrow.

"No, I'm …" Faye pauses, almost checking the *No* box, then stops.

"Faye Weston. You? *Not* being selective?"

"Fine. *Yes*," she whispers and checks at the same time. "Let's move on. Next question. Are you new to the area?"

119

"No."

"Really busy at work?"

"Yes."

"Looking for the life of the party?"

Joel considers her. "No," he says.

"You don't think I'd go for the life of the party?"

"No way. That wouldn't impress you. You'd want someone more ... toned down. And ... *just so*."

"Fair enough. Next. Are you emotional about love?"

Joel straightens and leans against the bench back. He looks at Faye beside him. She's focused on her questionnaire; her pen is poised over the paper. Finally, she looks at him. They're inches apart. A cold breeze blows wisps of her hair.

"Are you?" he asks.

"Well, you're doing pretty good with my answers, Joel."

"Yeah, but ... emotional about love? I just can't read you."

Faye looks at him for a quiet second. "Have a *hunch?*"

"I guess." He pauses a moment. "Because love is something *you* wouldn't take lightly. You'd ... well, you'd scrutinize it—that's your way. Which means you'd compare different aspects of love—rate them, critique them. Honesty, connection, desire ... each would be considered. So, yeah—I'm thinking you'd be emotional about love. Probably leaning toward analytical."

Her smile is slight, but genuine. *"Yep. You're good,"* she whispers, then checks the *Yes* box. "And hey," Faye says, setting down her pen and sipping her coffee. "Question for you. Why are *you* so into this?"

"Easy. Because it's not *for* me. There's no pressure this way."

"Well, I can print out another questionnaire. Get you added to Sadie's list." When she pauses, a few leaves swirl past. A car drives by. "Because you seem really ... *interested*, Joel."

"Give me that," he quickly says, reaching for her questionnaire. She hands over the pen, too, then sits back on the tree bench and cups her coffee close.

Now Joel scans the remaining questions and moves to the open-ended section. He reads a few about relationship goals and deal-breakers.

"Look at that." Faye leans over and points to a question. "They only give me *three* lines to explain an ideal partner?"

"Keep it brief, Weston."

"Okay. I'll give you three *words*. Hardworking ... Considerate ..."

With his pen hovering, Joel looks at her beside him. And waits for the third word. If he's not mistaken, Faye's eyes slightly glisten. So this Merry Match thing is getting to her.

*"Real,"* she barely says then.

Joel fills in the blank, whispering the word as he does. "And how are you going to find this superman?" he asks, looking at Faye again.

"I'm not. Sadie is."

"Okay, we'll see."

Again, Faye leans close. Their arms touch as she points to the questionnaire. "There's a good one. What's something people would be surprised to know about you?"

"*Hm.*" Joel looks from the question to her. Tips his head, too. "Looks particularly ravishing in a Pilgrim costume?"

Faye shoves him and says no more.

So Joel moves on to another question. "What didn't work well in your last relationship?"

She's quiet beside him, until finally he hears her answer.

"Me," she sadly admits.

Joel sets down the pen. His voice is level. He means what he's saying. "I find that hard to believe."

"What?"

"That it was *you*. To be honest, I find it hard to believe that you're not attached to some lucky guy. That you weren't scooped up long ago with a ring on your finger. That you're not married to someone with a *very* happy Meatloaf Monday every week."

Again, Faye just looks at him. Gives a small smile, too. "Here's the thing. I *was* seriously involved with a guy—for all the wrong reasons."

"Like what?"

"Like I jumped headfirst into the relationship shortly after my mother died. It was a rash decision, definitely. And, I don't know. Maybe I was looking to fill the void of my mother's loss. But what happened is that I let *him* fill it—with his decisions, opinions, plans. And *that* was a mistake because I kind of lost *my* self. So we didn't last." Faye looks out on the little green there. A squirrel scampers past; someone's walking a dog on the far end. "But it really scared me—once the relationship was over and the damage was done." Her voice drops now. "Scared me how I could make *such* a wrong … choice. So I really started working on my *own* sense of self after that. My own independence. Discovering who *I* am. Which is why I was devastated when I lost my beautiful apartment. I was also losing some of the identity I'd been rebuilding."

"Faye."

She looks at him now. Her smile's gone.

"Life," he quietly says, "tends to teach us the hard way. But hey, you're doing all right."

"And you're a good friend, Joel. Thanks for listening," she tells him while taking back her questionnaire. "Think I'll finish this later."

Joel nods. Stands, too. "Come on, I'll walk you home." He takes their empty coffee cups and tosses them in a nearby trash can. When he turns around, Faye's silently waiting for him. So on their short November walk, he tries to make her feel better.

"It's not so bad what you're doing, Faye. Putting yourself out there like that with Merry Match." He looks at her beside him. "Takes courage, actually."

"Maybe."

Walking along Winter Road, fallen autumn leaves crunch beneath their feet. And that November breeze rustles a lone straw scarecrow tied to a lamppost. When Joel glances over at Faye, she turns up the collar of her plaid jacket—right before they veer off to their own separate yards.

# *sixteen*

LATE TUESDAY AFTERNOON, JOEL CUTS out of work early. Thanksgiving is two days away and he's got a house to straighten up. Food to prep.

And a towering evergreen tree needing last-minute tending in his front yard. In the twilight, shadows are growing long. But there's enough sunlight to rake up the windblown leaves that accumulated around that tree.

Enough light, too, to decipher someone in those November shadows.

"Joel!" a voice calls out.

Joel squints through the low light. It's Faye, at her mailbox. She hesitates, then walks to his yard. Her hands clutch a few envelopes. It's obvious she just got home from work, too. She's got on a pale brown moto jacket over a fitted white top and long pleated navy skirt. The skirt reaches just about to her brown suede ankle boots.

"If I don't see you, Joel," she's saying while crossing

124

his lawn, "I wanted to wish you a happy Thanksgiving."

"You, too, Weston." Joel leans against his bamboo rake. "Got any plans?"

"Going to my dad's." Faye stops near the fir tree. She reaches over and sweeps her fingers across the soft green needles. "Some aunts and uncles will be there, too. Cousins. You know …"

"Sure. The family all together."

"What about you?" Faye asks then.

"I'm hosting here."

"Really!"

Joel nods and glances back at his farmhouse. Some of the windows glow with lamplight. "I always have my family here for Thanksgiving. Everyone helps, brings a dish or two. Then we make a big thing about lighting up the tree here to start the holiday season."

Faye steps back and eyes that towering tree—top to bottom. "Now *that's* quite a Trouble Tree."

"Not a Trouble Tree. I try not to bring my troubles home." Joel walks closer, leans back some and looks at the tree, too. "This here's just a plain old Christmas tree."

"And a grand one at that." Faye gives a wave, then. "I won't keep you. Have a good night, Joel."

"Yeah," he says, watching her go—and nodding when she looks back over her shoulder at him. "Got to get the house ready for company."

As Faye gets closer to her own yard, she blends in with the long shadows. And for a passing moment, before Joel loses sight of her, he thinks he'll do it. He'll just invite her over for Thanksgiving *dessert*. So he walks in her direction, raises a hand and calls out, "*Wait!* Faye!"

Right as he's saying it, Faye's already turning. And *really* smiling. "I know!" she calls back to him. "I just heard it. The night eagle!"

"Oh. No, I mean … I was going …" He gives a regretful shake of his head. And instead of saying, *Stop by Thanksgiving night, why don't you? Have a piece of pumpkin pie with me,* he says, "The owl? Not sure I heard it."

"Too bad." She's stopped on her lawn and looking toward the trees behind her bungalow. "It was a good hoot. Must've got lost in the wind."

Joel, just standing there with his rake, watches her. She's looking at him now, too. At the same time, they both start talking in that awkward pause—until they suddenly stop.

And Faye gives a quick smile.

And each of them simply turns away.

# *seventeen*

THANKSGIVING EVENING, FAYE DRIVES ALONG Winter Road. The country homes are lit up. Cars line the driveways. She slows her own car and glances in some house windows. In a sprawling ranch, a lantern-chandelier glows over a large dining room table. People linger around food and drink. In another home, an older couple stands on a front porch. They wave goodbye to a car just backing out of their driveway. Everywhere Faye looks, the holiday holds on. In living room windows around a large-screen TV. In another dining room illuminated and filled with a glittering chandelier and crystal glasses held high in a holiday toast.

But as she approaches Joel's farmhouse, she slows a little more. The absolutely beautiful, illuminated evergreen tree does it. The sight of that glimmering tree is breathtaking in the night. She continues on past, right as Joel's front door opens and a pool of lamplight spills onto the farmhouse porch.

By the time Faye's parked at her own house, she can see that Joel's whole family is on his porch. Some are hugging him goodbye. Some are already heading down the stairs toward the driveway. Faye lingers on the stoop of her bungalow and silently watches from the dark shadows. Another person hugs Joel now—it looks like maybe his mother. His brother, Brett, is there. A woman near him holds a toddler. All their muffled voices—their goodbyes, their casual, affectionate comments—carry in the night. Faye hears the happiness, the comfort, in their tone.

She feels a little something, too. Standing in her entry alcove and watching, there's some twinge in her heart. She feels it still as a car backs out of Joel's driveway and someone waves out the open window.

*"Ach,"* Faye says, turning away suddenly. *"It's the holidays,"* she whispers as she unlocks her own door and goes inside. *"Got me feeling sentimental, that's all."*

⁓

An hour later, it happens.

Of course it also happens when Faye's in her thermal jogger pajamas and lying snug under a throw on her couch. The only light on is her stained-glass teapot lamp—now sitting atop her new gray end table. Well, there's that light and the glow of the TV she's watching.

Which is when her cell phone rings.

She lifts it off the coffee table and hesitates when she sees who's calling. Then she smiles and answers.

"Joel?" she asks.

"You hungry, Weston?"

"It's Thanksgiving. I ate all day," she vaguely says while watching *It's a Wonderful Life* on her TV. George Bailey is trying like the dickens to get out of Bedford Falls and see the world.

"Yeah, but you didn't *really* eat," Joel's saying.

"I didn't?"

"No. Because you see ... At your dad's table today, when the folks all asked about your new house, and your job, and when you're getting married, and are you seeing anybody, you kind of moved the food around on your plate. And talked about work, and *maybe* your upcoming Merry Match dates. Or ... or you tried to deflect back to them so they forgot they even asked about you and why you didn't bring someone to Thanksgiving dinner. So," Joel says, pauses, then goes on, "you didn't *really* eat."

"It's uncanny." Faye sits up and pulls the knit throw over her lap. "How do you know all this?"

"Because that's what *I* just did. So what are you doing now?"

"Watching TV."

"*It's a Wonderful Life?* On CT-TV?"

Faye turns up her hand. "Yes!"

"Me, too. I always like this part when George and Mary throw rocks at the old Granville house."

"So do I. But I agree with Mary. That dilapidated home still has such beauty in it. Such ... *romance*," Faye says, her voice drifting off as she watches the movie scene. "I mean, look at that forlorn turreted Victorian."

Faye's quiet, then. Joel is, too, as George shatters a window and makes his hopeful, rambling wish—all while

Mary just watches. His wish goes on and on until Mary scoops up a rock. She heaves it and breaks a window, too, before making her own silent wish.

"If *you* could throw a rock at the old Granville house," Joel's voice asks through the phone, "what would your wish be, Faye?"

"Me?" Faye looks toward her own paned window. Darkness presses against the glass on this cold November night. "I don't know. Maybe … maybe to see one of your night eagles swoop through the shadows outside. That'd be pretty special."

There's some silence before Joel answers. "Yeah. Good one."

"What about you, Joel? What would you wish for?" Faye asks in her dimly lit family room.

"Easy. That you would just come over. We'll have a turkey sandwich and piece of pie and watch the movie together."

Faye lifts that throw and looks at what she's wearing. "I'm in my pajamas."

"Me, too," Joel says right back.

"You are *not* in your pajamas."

"Am too."

"You're so full of it."

"Fine." George Bailey's voice fills a quiet pause. "I'm in my sweats," Joel finally admits. "And apparently you don't want any of the amazing leftovers sitting here."

*"Oh!"* Faye tosses aside that warm, cozy knitted throw. "Be there in ten minutes."

"*Shoot!*" Joel says as he flies up the stairs to his bedroom. On the way down the hall, he's whipping off his button-down and kicking off his chukka boots. In his bedroom, he grabs his jogger sweatpants and a long-sleeve thermal tee from his dresser, gets out of his black jeans and puts all that other stuff on. His fisherman cardigan, too, which he puts on over it all. Lastly, he steps into his suede moccasin slippers.

And fifteen minutes later, he's settled in the dining room like he never made that mad, panicked dash through his house.

Like he was never winded.

Like his heart never raced.

No, all's good now as he and Faye sit at the dining room table and make turkey sandwiches while the TV blasts from the living room. Oh, and he can't help smiling at what's between them on the table. When he opened his door to Faye earlier, she stood on his porch and offered a Thanksgiving centerpiece for their sandwich rendezvous— her fluffy, stuffed Pilgrim-turkey from bingo night.

"Now, I like *just* turkey—white meat, sliced thin," Faye says, forking a few cut pieces off a platter. "With cheese and mayo. Oh, and a dot of mustard," she adds, squeezing a few dots on her turkey—sliced thin—all laid out on her already-toasted bread. "And for the mayo?" She reaches a knife into the mayonnaise jar. "A healthy slather." Carefully, but firmly, she sets the top slice of toasted bread onto her sandwich and pats it. "What about you?"

"Me?" Joel looks across the table at her. Faye's sitting there in red-and-black buffalo-plaid thermal pajamas. She wears a long sherpa-lined cardigan-sweatshirt over it all.

"I pretty much like a whole turkey-dinner sandwich." He lifts his top slice of bread and tips his plate to reveal the turkey slices, thin layer of stuffing *and* cranberry sauce there—topped with gravy. Patting his sandwich closed, he looks over at her. "Warmed in the microwave."

"Huh, that *does* sound good." She picks up the knife and carefully cuts her bread—on the diagonal. Trims the crust, too. "Want me to cut yours? Make it all—"

"Just so." Joel slides his plate across the table. "But I *only* want it cut. Leave the crust. And take a hunk for yourself. See how it stacks up against yours."

Then ... after the microwaving and drink-pouring and napkin-grabbing, the TV trays come out. In the living room now, Faye settles on one end of a large L-shaped sofa; Joel sits on the other end. They adjust the throw pillows and pull over their food trays and dig in.

"What's the consensus?" Joel asks as Faye samples his loaded sandwich wedge.

"Yours is *good*," she says around a mouthful.

"But ..."

"Mine is better."

Joel tosses up his hands. *"What?"*

"Yes, because in *my* sandwich? You can really taste and appreciate the savory turkey flavor—which gets lost in the mishmash of yours." To have him see for himself, Faye walks to *his* couch-end with a wedge of her simple sandwich. Both his hands are holding his *mega* sandwich, so she puts her wedge to his mouth. "Take it," she says, feeding it to him.

Unable to talk, he just nods while chewing.

"Well?" she asks when he finally downs it.

"What can I say? Yours is a ... chick sandwich. Mine is a guy's."

*"Ooh. Fine."* Faye settles on the couch again and turns to the TV. "Wait." She motions to a tall table lamp. "Can you dim that?" she asks. "I like it dark when I watch a movie."

Joel reaches over and dims the table lamp, leaving just enough light to eat by. "Good?" he asks.

Faye nods.

They keep eating, then. And quiet down. And resume watching *It's a Wonderful Life.* They analyze some scenes, go silent during others—all while working on their hefty sandwiches compensating for what they *didn't* get to eat around the Thanksgiving table earlier.

When Faye finishes, she moves aside her TV tray, slips off her shearling-lined suede ankle boots, pulls her thick cable-knit black socks up over her plaid thermal pajama bottoms and stretches out on her part of the sofa. "May I?" she asks, tugging a fringed throw off the sofa back.

Joel nods and works on his sandwich. White twinkle lights glimmer on the mantel. A wind kicks up outside the paned windows. A basket of cut firewood sits near the fireplace. An amber pillar candle flickers in a vintage lantern on a wall shelf.

All the while, they're drawn into Bedford Falls. And watch George Bailey's life come undone on the screen. During a commercial, Joel asks Faye if she wants some pumpkin pie.

"Of course!" As she says it, she sits up on the couch.

"Warm? Or chilled?"

"Warm. And ... oh, wait." She tosses off that throw

and walks in her stocking feet after him to the kitchen. "I like whipped cream on it, too," she calls out.

"What about ice cream?"

"One scoop. But to the side. Not *on* the pie—because the warm pie will melt it too fast."

Joel turns on the coffeemaker and slides the pie in the oven. "Just for a few minutes," he says, lifting two plates from the cupboard and setting them on the island. Faye sits on a stool there and watches as he opens the cutlery drawer next. He lifts out a few pieces, then stops and looks at her. "Important question now. Spoon?" he asks, lifting one. "Or fork?"

"Spoon. To mush it all together."

Joel laughs. "You better run all these questions by your blind dates, Faye."

She laughs, too. Her eyes crinkle as she does, as she leans back on that stool, and smiles, and mentions how those dates start up soon.

Minutes later, they're back in the living room.

Back on their respective sofa cushions.

Pie plates are balanced on laps now.

Coffee cups sit on end tables.

Night has fallen outside.

A gust of wind rattles the windowpanes.

In the black-and-white movie on the TV, a desperate George Bailey talks to his guardian angel, Clarence.

Shadows in Joel's living room grow long.

Faye's soft voice murmurs.

Joel answers, and looks over at her.

And tells her it's been a really nice Thanksgiving.

# *eighteen*

ALL OF ADDISON MUST HAVE the same idea Joel has—to get an early start on Christmas shopping. Because it's Saturday afternoon of Thanksgiving weekend and he can barely move on the town green. The Merry Market is up and running. Tents and booths are crowded together. Some booths are strung with blinking lights; others have garland looped across the top; some sell crafts; others sell food; others sell clothes and goods. All of them are mobbed. Beneath cloudy skies, there's a sea of hats and scarves and coats and parkas swirling all around.

But Joel presses forward. The holiday season will be busy at the tavern and he has to squeeze in his shopping like this. So he tugs his wool beanie lower and soldiers on.

And stops at a very familiar and unexpected booth—Silver Settings.

Inside the booth, sample place settings with dishes and flatware are arranged on a few tables. Fold-up chairs are set in front of each so that customers can … *simulate*. Posters on the wall display more flatware styles.

And all of it is helmed by Faye. She's just finishing with a customer.

"Excuse me, miss," Joel says while pointing to a display chart hung in the background. "Can you please suggest which handle goes best with my face?" He picks up a fork from the samples laid out in the booth. "Brushed silver?" He raises another higher. "Gold?"

Faye warmly smiles. "What are you doing here?" As she asks, she's pulling on a gold beret matching the honey-gold plaid wool jacket she wears over black leggings and lace-up duck boots.

"Knocked off early from work," Joel explains when she walks closer. "The tavern's hopping, and my father *loves* catching up with the Thanksgiving weekend crowd. So between him and my bartender Kevin, they've got the joint covered. I'll head back and close up tonight. But for now?" Joel turns and gazes out at the merchant booths circling The Green. "I do *this* every year."

"This?" Faye asks, tucking a thick scarf around her neck.

"I attempt some Christmas shopping here *every* Thanksgiving weekend. But I'm usually at a total loss and end up buying gift cards."

"Oh, no."

"Afraid so."

"But Joel. That's so … impersonal."

He turns up his hands.

"Listen. I'm done for the day. My coworker, Gloria, is covering the afternoon shift," Faye says while nodding to another woman in the booth. "So maybe I can help you."

"Hey, that'd be great. If you're sure, Weston."

"I am." She grabs her purse and turns back to him. "Now who are you shopping for?"

Well … In no time, he's shopping for no one. Not after stops with Faye at many of the booths: Circa 1765 Antiques, Near and Deer Wood Carvings, Vagabond Vintage, The Clock Shop and Felucca's Fine Gifts. Joel's never been loaded down with so many stuffed shopping bags in his whole life. While a clerk rings him out at one booth, he picks up a nearby pale-gray ceramic pitcher. It's chipped with age, but is tall—in a contemporary way. "Hipstoric, no? Marries the old with a modern look?" he asks Faye.

She gives an assured nod. "Oh, I *like* that one. I'm going to treat myself."

After Faye makes her purchase and they leave that booth, Joel glances at his list—which is all crossed out.

"You good now?" Faye asks, standing close by. From beneath that gold beret, her blonde hair sweeps her shoulders.

"I'm *done* now," he tells her, pocketing his list. He looks at her and shakes his head, too. "How do you do it?"

"Do what?"

"I gave you the *briefest* description of my family and some friends. And you turned into a Christmas-gift whisperer." He holds up his several bags laden with merchandise and spilling with tufts of holiday wrapping tissue.

"Aww, Joel. I had fun shopping with you."

They cross the busy street to the tavern—where they're both parked nearby.

"Seriously, Faye. These presents can't be topped," he tells her as he deposits the shopping bags inside his pickup truck. "Listen." Joel turns then. People mill past them. A snow flurry swirls from the late-afternoon November sky. And Faye stands there waiting in her gold coat and beret. "How can I ever thank you?" he asks her.

*"Hmm."* Faye tips her head as she squints at him through those falling snowflakes. "I think I know just the way."

⌐∾○

Strings of white bulbs crisscross over Cooper Hardware's tree lot. Fraser firs and blue spruces and balsam firs lean against wood railings. Decorated wreaths with red velvet bows hang from a large display. After stopping at the hot cocoa booth, they veer to the trees.

"How about this one?" Joel's asking five minutes later. As he does, he tamps a Christmas tree stump on the frozen ground.

Sipping her hot chocolate, Faye backs up and discreetly scrutinizes Joel first. He looks downright handsome in his black canvas bomber open over a button-down and army-green cargo pants with black work boots. His dark hair curls from beneath his wool beanie. A shadow of whiskers covers his jaw.

*Just friends,* she silently reminds herself. *So back to the task at hand.* Which is analyzing the third Christmas tree Joel just pulled from the rails at Cooper Hardware's tree lot. Still not quite right, so she shakes her head.

"What about this one?" he asks, swapping out the tree for another.

"Too wide."

And the adjectives continue as they work their way down a long line of leaning trees.

Too skinny.

Scrawny.

Tall.

Short.

Squat.

Misshapen.

In the third row of trees, Joel lifts a Fraser fir that Faye studies. She also removes a glove and sweeps her bare fingers across the blue-green needles.

Joel smiles as he watches her intense tree-selection process. "You know. If you're going to be as particular about your blind dates as you are with a Christmas tree, Faye ... well, good luck to the gents."

She swats him with her clutched glove, then puts it back on and finishes her hot cocoa. "This will be my *first* Christmas tree in my *first* house, so I want it to be ..." She pauses while surveying the trees around them.

"I know," Joel quietly says. "Just so."

And the next one is. It's a balsam fir, five feet tall.

"The tree's a *beautiful* shade of green," Faye vaguely comments. "And it's ... an elegant, slim shape."

So they take it. After it's netted and paid for, Faye turns to him. "What about you? Don't you want a tree?"

"I've got all the tree I need outside," he says while they cross Cooper Hardware's parking lot. When Joel hefts her tree into his truck bed, he tells her, "So I just light up a ceramic number inside. And put candles in the windows. It's enough," he says, closing the tailgate. "You *can* help me pick out the perfect wreath, though."

⁓

But if Joel Briggs thought that picking out a Christmas tree and wreath was a finicky ordeal, he had no idea what lay in store.

Had no idea that once they set Faye's balsam fir in her tree stand, he'd be standing alone in her bungalow living room. As she heads outside—where she'll apparently have a passerby-view of her tree—he looks around the room. There's that hipstoric vibe she's after—an old, distressed wooden trunk coffee table beside a silver-gray sofa with sleek, modern lines. A plush abstract area rug of mottled golds, blues, grays and sage greens over the original dark hardwood floor. Table lamps and candles on the mantel cast a glow on it all.

"A little to the left," Faye calls in now through her open living room window.

So he does it. Joel shifts her tree stand left.

"No," she quickly says. "My left. Not yours."

So he adjusts the tree placement. "How about this?" he calls back while bending to see her through the window. The light outside is dusky now, just after sunset. Tiny snowflakes swirl down in another flurry, too. Those snowflakes land on her shoulder and dust her gold-plaid coat.

Faye shakes her head. "Maybe you had it before. Can you put it where it was?"

He does. He shifts that tree there, here, closer. At one point, he motions to his watch. "I have to get back to work later," he reminds her.

Funny, though. Joel never checks that watch again as Faye's dithering and he's tree-turning. He does pause, though, and ventures outside for a look in, too. The tree is perfectly centered in her drapery-lined picture window. He turns to Faye still standing there. The snow dusts even her gold beret now. "I think your tree looks beautiful, Faye."

She looks from him—to her tree on the other side of that window. "I just can't tell. Maybe once the lights are on it." Again, she looks to him. "Would you help me string them?"

And he does.

Joel doesn't fight her on any of it.

Not on the lights; nor the tree angle; nor the windows' drapery adjustment.

Doesn't resist at all on this unexpected November afternoon spent with his amusing, fussy—but always right—neighborhood friend.

He especially doesn't fight the smile on his face when an hour later he's moving the lit, now-*twinkling* tree—just a smidge to the right—in the expansive front paned window of Faye Weston's beloved country bungalow.

# *nineteen*

JUST LIKE THAT, IT'S DECEMBER.

And after the first weekend of the month, Faye thinks it's as if a switch got flicked. Addison is more enchanting than ever. There are glowing Christmas lights everywhere—around shop fronts, on the town tree at The Green, atop hedges and entwined in white picket fences.

Candles glimmer in paned windows of grand historic colonials and clapboard-sided Cape Cods.

Cornstalks at lampposts have been replaced with balsam garland wrapped in twinkling white lights—including at Silver Settings' entryway. Small white bulbs are also strung beneath the eaves of the building's Craftsman-style portico. A large balsam wreath hangs on the door; a nutcracker statue stands sentry on the stoop.

Faye's working at the front lobby desk Tuesday morning when that entry door opens and Vera Sterling walks in.

"We decided on a style, Faye," Vera says, walking to the desk. She's carrying a small box of flatware samples, which she sets on the countertop. "We're going with the *Cedar Lace* pattern for our reception," she goes on, loosening her scarf and pulling off a pair of leather gloves. "That *really* delicate cedar leaf design on the fiddleback shape gives it just the look we want."

"Oh, what a stunning choice." Faye lifts out a *Cedar Lace* spoon and fork and sets them on the countertop. "Simplicity at its finest. And the good news is that we have this all in stock, so I'll reserve it for you right away."

"And you have Frank Lombardo's number at the Addison Boathouse?"

"I do." Faye confirms the final guest head count with Vera. "I'll call Frank and coordinate a drop-off time there before your wedding."

"Saturday, December 16."

Faye looks up from the notes she's jotting. "*Ooh*, getting close. You must be so excited."

"We are! Derek and I are really ready for this."

Faye sets down her pen and places the flatware samples back in the box. "You know, I was at Cooper Hardware Thanksgiving weekend, actually. Picked out my Christmas tree there. It's a beautiful one, too."

"Derek's got the best trees. And Faye, you've been beyond helpful to us," Vera is saying as she pulls something from her purse. "So Derek and I would like to have you at our wedding *and* reception." She sets a formal invitation on the countertop.

Faye picks up the cream-colored card embossed in cursive font—the scrolls nearly matching the flatware design. She whispers aloud some of the details, too. *"Candlelit marriage ceremony at the Snowflakes and Coffee Cakes barn at Addison Cove."* Her eyes skim the date and time. *"Reception to follow at Addison Boathouse."*

"You'll get to see your gorgeous silverware all decked out beside our lantern centerpieces." Vera's putting on her gloves now. "And bring a guest, please!"

Faye looks up from the invitation. "We'll see," she says with a smile. "Regardless, I wouldn't miss it, Vera."

And if all goes well, Faye muses after walking Vera to the door, *maybe* one of her Merry Match dates will accompany her to the big event.

You never know … First date's tonight.

Joel's behind the bar that evening. Addison's Merry Match has just begun, and he needs to oversee its opening night at his tavern. A tray of clean and sparkling glasses sits on the bar, and he lines them on a shelf until someone says his name. So he turns and is surprised to see Faye. Wearing her gold-plaid coat, she's headed his way.

"Hey, Weston," Joel says while buffing a glass with a dry cloth. "What can I get you?"

"Nothing, yet," Faye tells him as she sits at a stool and scans the bar. "My first date's tonight, and I have to get ready."

"And where's this big date happening?"

*"Here."* Faye turns to him now. "You said this was one of the hosting spots, right? I mean, you've got the candy-cane heart in your window. *And* hearts for the Merry

Match date tables." She nods to a few heart figurines lined up on the bar.

"Wow." Joel sets the polished glass on the shelf and picks up another to buff. "I never thought you'd choose *this* place."

"Why not?"

"Because you haven't been here much. Except for my silverware order, and maybe a lunch. And that historical tour."

"Which convinced me this was the *perfect* place."

"Why's that?" Joel asks, setting that now-shined glass aside.

"I'll tell you why." Faye loosens her plaid coat. "Joel's is perfect for my dates because you have *everything* here. Coffee for an afternoon date. Wine for evening dates. Meals if we want. And it's the kind of place that's easy in, easy out."

"What do you mean?"

"Well, if all goes okay, my date and I can take a walk across the street to The Green. Stop at the Christmas tree there. Browse the Merry Market booths."

Joel folds back the cuffs of his white button-down. "And if the date *doesn't* go well?"

"Like I said, easy." Faye motions to the doorway. "We can politely walk to our respective cars parked outside and ... leave."

Joel notices that as Faye says all this, her nerves show. She tucks back her hair. Shifts her coat. Turns on the stool. "Well, I'm wishing you luck, Faye. But you seem a little nervous," he goes on, putting a few more clean glasses on the long shelf behind the bar. "You sure you're okay with all this?"

145

"*Ach,* I don't know, Joel," she says, leaning an elbow on the bar. "I feel *really* nervous, actually. And to be honest?" she continues, squinting at him now. "That's another reason I picked your tavern for my dates."

"I don't get it."

"It's just that … if the date's not going well and I want out, maybe you can assist?"

"Of course. Don't worry about it." Joel slides aside his empty glass tray now. "That's what friends are for."

"*Phew.* I'm so relieved." Faye stands then and walks to a table kind of near the door *and* a window. "Oh, and one more thing," she says, turning back to him.

"Name it."

Standing beside that table, she gently pats it. "I'd like to reserve *this* table for *each* date."

"Wait a minute." Joel, still behind the bar, leans both elbows on it and squints at her across the room. "*All* your dates will be here?"

"Yes."

"You don't want to schedule a date at the dance studio and take a foxtrot lesson? Or … have a milkshake at the general store soda fountain?" He turns up his hands. "There's a whole list of potential Merry Match stops."

"And mine are all here. If that's all right, I mean?"

"It is. Whatever you want."

"Okay, good." Faye adjusts a chair at *her* table. "I want each date in the *same* place—for comparison. That way, the venue stays the same. The talk does, too. Kind of. And the atmosphere is the same. Just the guy changes. Because I have a set of questions," she says as she circles that table. "And I have to assess my dates' answers—so the

146

environment remains constant. If it didn't, you know, if I was, say, on a Cooper Hardware carriage ride next time, well, that might skew my comparisons."

"You don't find that a bit ... technical?"

"Well. Yes. That's the whole point."

"Only you, Faye," he says with a half smile. After picking up one of the candy-cane heart figurines, he walks to *Faye Weston's* table and sets down the Merry Match heart. He can't hide that he's amused, then, as she hovers nearby. So he steps back and crosses his arms. "Well, I'm also available for feedback," he says. "And to listen to any horror stories. You just sit at the Trouble Tree afterward," he goes on, nodding to the artificial fir tree on the bar, "and tell me what's troubling about the date. Oh, and I can chime in, too. *If* you want an outside opinion."

Faye nudges her tabletop heart to the side. "You *still* have no faith this can work."

"No, I don't. Feel free to prove me wrong, though. Because I *am* pulling for you, Weston. But for me? It's too ... arranged. With too many expectations." Joel looks to the tavern's six-panel wooden entrance door. "And where is this Mr. Wonderful, anyway?"

"He's not here yet. I arrived early to get my table," she says while slipping off her coat. "And get situated. I like to be prepared."

Joel nods and heads back to the bar. Once there, he looks over and sees Faye hanging her coat on the back of her Windsor chair. She dressed casual for this date—a loose sleeveless beige sweater over an untucked white blouse and black skinny pants. Black Chelsea boots, too. Heavy gold hoop earrings are her only jewelry. Her whole look is simple, but all class.

And as he wipes down the bar, and takes an order from a waitress, and mixes two drinks for customers, he also glances over at Faye angling her chair this way, then that. And fussing with napkins on the table. Turning that candy-cane heart figurine. Touching her water glass.

He laughs to himself, too. What is it about this woman that charms him? Of *course* methodical Faye would show up for her dates at the same place, same table, with the same setup. Because if Joel knows anything about precise Faye Weston and her numbered life list, and her meticulous meatloaf, and her no-nonsense wheelie mobile office—it wouldn't be any other way.

⁓

But some things you can't *be* methodical about. Can't handle with precision.

Things like meeting a blind date.

Ten minutes later, Joel discreetly watches that happen. Some dude walks into the tavern, spots the candy-cane figurine on Faye's table and heads over. His and Faye's awkwardness is obvious as they greet one another. As Faye half stands, but he kindly motions her down. As they sort of clumsily shake hands rather than give a light hug. As the guy sits and nods in a moment of silence.

So after straightening his black vest over his white shirt, Joel walks to their date table. Oh, and he can't miss Faye's disguised relief upon seeing him headed her way.

"Good evening, folks," Joel says, not letting on that he and Faye are friends. "What can I get you tonight?" After taking their drink orders—a draft beer and glass of white wine—he asks, "Can I interest you in the Merry Match special? It's on the house for our dates."

"That'd be *sweet*," the dude tells him. He looks to be in his mid-thirties. His hair is short; his face, clean-shaven. He's taking off his wool peacoat as he talks, then hanging it on his chair. "This is our first date, actually," he adds, motioning across the table to Faye, then clearing his throat.

"Excuse me, but what, exactly, *is* the date special?" Faye asks Joel.

"An appetizer tonight. Tater-tot cups. Which are mini tater-tot muffins topped with cheddar cheese, sour cream, crumbled bacon and some green onion."

"Sounds great," the date says.

"Okay. Your waitress will bring a platter with your drinks." As Joel turns away, he slaps the guy's shoulder. "Good luck, cowboy," he tells him.

When he walks back to the bar, Joel also can't miss Faye glaring at him. He sees it in the glow of the blinking neon Christmas bell in the tavern's front window.

⁀◌

"No, no, no, no—*no*."

"That good?" Joel asks when Faye later lands on a barstool with her proclamation.

"Well, for a *positive* spin?" she goes on while tugging off her gold-plaid coat *again*. "I just checked number nine off my life list."

"Can't wait to hear this one," Joel says over his shoulder while pulling a draft beer.

"Number nine: Don't be afraid to say no to people. Which I just did. I said no and declined a second date."

"That was fast." After sliding the beer to a waiting customer, Joel wipes his fingers on a cloth and turns to Faye. "But I saw you two walk out together. Thought you were maybe taking a stroll around The Green. See the town Christmas tree up close."

"No. He walked me to my car. Then he walked to his. Then I waved as he took off. And then? I promptly came back in here." She leans back on her barstool. "And here I am. At the Trouble Tree."

"What *happened?*"

"Nothing." Faye gazes at the Trouble Tree on the bar. Instead of the harvest orange, tiny *white* lights glimmer in its green boughs now. "Except he ate the whole plate of tater-tot cups."

"Get out!"

Faye nods. "He did. I ate one, and he … well … he chowed down. Just nodded and popped one after every question I asked him. You know …" she explains, tucking back her blunt-cut blonde hair. "What do you do for a living? Favorite music? Glass half-empty or half-full kind of person? He mumbled out his answers and left the rest to me."

"Faye." Joel steps closer from behind the bar. "Did you even give him a *chance* to talk?"

"I *did*. But he took some remote work-from-home job a year ago. And let me tell you, Joel. Social isolation has done him *no* favors. He couldn't really converse."

"Come on. You didn't want dinner? Maybe he'd loosen up over a meal?"

"No. We stopped at the appetizer. So here I am." She glances back through the shadowed bar, past the patrons, and two other Merry Match date tables, then back to Joel. "Remind me again why I'm doing this?"

Joel watches her. And draws a hand down his whiskered jaw. "Number twenty on your list."

*"Fall in love,"* Faye sadly whispers. "Why does it have to be so hard?" She reaches to the Trouble Tree's ornament bowl, too, and lifts a mini glittered bell. "I see you swapped out the acorns?"

"For the Christmas season," Joel says. "And chin up, Weston. That was just your first date. Give it a chance."

*"I will,"* she sighs.

"There'll be some gem in there. You'll see."

"At this rate, I can probably hang four or five glitter ornaments on your Trouble Tree." She delicately hangs the one she picked, a red glitter bell, on a green bough. "For all my dates ahead."

⟡

Once Joel's back home later, he stops on his front porch. The night is cold and dark. He leans on the porch post and looks at the illuminated fir tree in the yard. Pulls his cargo jacket closed around him. A minute or two passes. All's quiet. Standing there, it hits him then. Another year's gone by, and he's still alone. Has no one he can stand with on his front porch—his arm around her shoulder in the cold of night—while looking together at his decorated tree.

There hasn't been someone for a long time now.

So he ends up standing out here by himself. Tonight, he thinks of the few Merry Match dates he witnessed earlier. The awkward talks. The smiles. The leaning close and laughing. The uncomfortable pauses. Call him old-fashioned ... sentimental ... nostalgic. *Whatever.* He gives the couples credit for trying—Faye included. Gives them credit for actively seeking out a connection. Some chance at something real.

But it's not for him, those blind-date setups. He holds out hope for some other way.

His thoughts are interrupted just then by an approaching car. As it nears his yard, the vehicle slows in front of his towering, festive evergreen tree. That happens a lot with townsfolk mesmerized by the sight.

"Heckuva tree, guy," the driver calls out his open window when he cruises past. "Real beauty!"

Joel gives a wave from the porch, and then—nothing.

Night has truly fallen and all is still. He stands there another minute. Breathes. Looks at the black sky dotted with tiny stars. In the distance, a single barred owl calls—the muffled sound lonely in the night.

# *twenty*

WEDNESDAY EVENING, FAYE STANDS AT her gray-swirled white kitchen island. Two baking pans are covered with uncooked cookies. *"Chef's kiss,"* she whispers, kissing her fingertips at the multiple rows of dough balls. For a festive look, she rolled some in red sugar grains, some green. Now, after whisking and beating and mixing one more bowl of cookie dough, she begins filling her last pan—after sliding a *filled* cookie sheet into the preheated oven.

Which is when her cell phone rings. So she puts it on speaker while shaping her cookies.

*"Well?"* Sadie gets right to it. "How'd your first date go last night? I'm *dying* to hear!"

"Oh, Sadie. Not good," Faye says, pressing a mounded scoop of dough into a ball. "The date was kind of a dud."

*"Aww.* With Sean? I'm sorry to hear this."

"Yeah." As she says it, Faye rolls her cookie dough ball

in a bowl of red sugar grains.

"I feel so bad. Me and my staff worked really hard on the matches."

"Well, sometimes things look different on paper." Faye pauses while lining up a few freshly sugar-rolled dough balls on her baking pan. "Hopefully, the next one will be better," she vaguely says.

"Hopefully. Now remind me, when *is* your next date?"

Another pause as Faye rolls a new scoop of dough in her hands. "Tomorrow. It's line-dancing night this time around."

"Oh, fun! But hey, you sound busy," Sadie's voice comes over the cell phone speaker. "What're you up to now?"

"Ha!" Another ball gets rolled in sugar, green grains this time. "I'm actually working on number seven on my life list—expertly cook something from scratch."

"*Ooh* … And what's cooking?"

"I'm baking peanut butter blossom cookies for a photo shoot at work tomorrow." The sweet aroma filling her kitchen gets Faye to glance at the oven timer. "We're taking pictures of a grandly set holiday table for the *Addison Weekly's Holiday Happenings* section. So don't mind me," Faye exclaims, now lining up chocolate kisses to press into the just-about-baked cookies in the oven. "Oh, Sadie! There's the timer, got to run!"

⤳

Thursday evening, Joel watches a transformation from behind the bar.

A holiday transformation.

Waitresses string up silver garland entwined with multicolored lights.

Kevin loops more garland over the gilded mirror behind the bar.

A waiter stacks Christmas records in the old jukebox.

And birch-log deer with twig antlers stand at either end of the bar.

Amidst it all, Faye arrives and takes off her coat at her regular window table. She's wearing a buffalo-plaid button-down tucked into skinny jeans. A wide leather belt is slung around her hips; those jeans are tucked into scuffed-up cowboy boots. Carefully, then, she hangs her coat over the back of her Windsor chair.

"Take two, huh?" Joel asks when he walks over and sets menus on the table.

"I'll give this another try, anyway," Faye ventures, then adjusts her chair to a certain, just-so angle. "There's a nice holiday vibe here tonight," she remarks, glancing at the newly hung garland swags, the twinkling Christmas lights. "So maybe this blind date will be better."

Joel nods to her cowboy boots. "And *you're* dressed to get your stomp on, I see."

"Yeah. I'm thinking that line-dancing together will be better than just watching someone eat."

"Hope so, Weston. Hang in there," Joel tells her, setting the Merry Match candy-cane heart on her table, too, before heading back to the bar. When he gets there, Kevin lets out a really low whistle. "What's up?" Joel asks him.

"Oh, man." Kevin nods to Faye standing and shaking

hands with her just-arriving date. "I'm glad I'm married and not going through that."

"I'll bet," Joel says, glancing Faye's way. "But I'll tell you, Kev. That Sadie knew what she was doing for small businesses with this Merry Match thing. The place has been hopping," he adds as a small crowd arrives at the painted-black entry door. "I guess love brings in the business."

"Yep." Kevin ties on a white bartending apron. "And if the dates don't work out, heartache always has a spot here at the bar."

◌

An hour passes in the tavern.

It's a busy night with the line-dancing crowd. The DJ works the room; music blasts; boots stomp. A sea of people moves around, talks at tables, sits at the bar. A waiter delivers a glass of wine and pitcher of beer to Faye and her date—who lifts the pitcher and fills his glass. Occasionally, Joel catches sight of the two of them talking at their table. Laughing, too. Faye's date lifts that pitcher again and tops off his glass. Leans in sometimes, chatting with Faye. He seems decent.

So when he gets a chance, Joel discreetly gives Faye a questioning thumbs-up. When her date turns away, she wavers her hand in a gesture indicating the guy's okay.

Which is why Joel's surprised at what he sees when Faye and her date get up to line-dance. At first, Joel thinks the guy just trips when he stands at the table. Still, from the bar, he keeps an eye on him in the crowd.

Good thing, too. Because once Faye and her date get to the dance floor, Joel gets another feeling. The guy's sloppy, like he maybe had one too many drinks. He slightly stumbles—right into Faye. And Faye's looking concerned now as she halfheartedly shuffles and pivots and stomps on the wooden floor.

So Joel pulls Kevin aside. They need to salvage the situation for Faye. Luckily, Joel's father just arrived with a basket of newly made whisk brooms for the tavern's New Year's celebration.

"Dad," Joel says now, catching up with his father. "I need a favor. Just set those brooms down," he quickly tells him while inching toward the dance floor, "and cover the bar for me and Kevin?"

"Sure. Something wrong?" his father calls out after setting the basket behind the bar.

"Patron needs some assistance," Joel answers before he and Kevin spot Faye's date in the mobbed room.

It happens in a quiet blur, then. Kevin and Joel move onto that dance floor in a way that no one really notices. But Faye catches Joel's eye, so he gives her a reassuring nod—right as Kevin discreetly pulls aside her date. Joel hears Kevin talk over the music.

"Come on, my friend," Kevin tells him as he takes the guy's arm. "Let's get some air outside."

The date doesn't fight him. He actually high-fives Kevin like he thinks he knows him. Man, he's worse off than Joel thought. Kevin goes along with the guy as they head to the exit.

But Joel's heading to Faye now. Left suddenly alone on the stompin' dance floor, she looks really uncomfortable.

But she stays with the dance, hesitantly turning this way, kicking and stepping, and turning once more—all while glancing over her shoulder.

And spotting Joel—right there.

Joel—matching her line-dancing steps move for move.

"Hey." He leans close, tugs down his black vest and shoves up his white shirtsleeves. "I'll get you through this. Just follow my lead."

Faye does as the DJ's record spins. She follows along with Joel as guitars twang and a drum keeps a pulsing beat.

As people move in unison around them on the dance floor.

As she and Joel slide and shuffle and stomp to the end of the song.

Afterward, though? She's still shook up. So Joel sits with her at her date table.

"He seemed *fine* earlier," Faye's saying. "He was okay. You know, talking. Laughing. I didn't even notice he was a little lit until he stood and lost his balance."

"Must've had a few before he even got here," Joel tells her.

Faye looks at him and shakes her head. "I'm *so* embarrassed."

"Don't be." He reaches over and squeezes her hand. "You did nothing wrong."

She gives a small smile then. "What happened to the guy?" she asks, glancing around. "Where'd he go?"

"Kevin took him outside and talked him down. Got him a taxi ride home." Joel turns up his hands. "At least he didn't resist."

Faye sighs, then lifts her gold-plaid coat off the chair. "I'm going to take off, too."

Joel stands with her. "Let me walk you out."

On the way, Joel swings by the bar and grabs one of those new mini corn brooms his father delivered. Once he and Faye leave through the six-panel black-painted door, Joel stops her on the cobblestone sidewalk.

"Here, let's whisk off the bad vibes of the night." As he says it, he whisks the air around her, brushes the night off her shoulders, her arms, and gets her laughing.

"Thanks, Joel," Faye tells him. "Nice to know I can count on you."

Joel backs up a step and nods. "Anytime, friend." He leans against the side of the low brick building now and crosses his arms. For a few minutes, they talk a little more before Faye wanders to her car parked at the curb.

"You going to hang in there with these dates?" Joel asks.

Faye's digging her keys out of her purse. She looks over at him. "Well, I'm not a quitter." Turning to her car, she says over her shoulder, "So I'll give it another go."

"All right." Joel hurries over and opens the car door for her. "Better luck next time, Weston." And after she gets in her car and buckles up, he taps her window. "Drive safe."

❧

Something about the night was actually alarming, though. Unsettling. So an hour later, Joel leaves the tavern in Kevin's hands and heads home. He calls Faye then, too.

"Joel?" she asks into the phone.

"Want to be sure you made it home okay."

"Yeah, I did." A pause, then, "Thanks."

"You all right? What are you up to now?"

"Feeling sorry for myself and drowning my sorrows in peanut butter blossoms."

"In *what?*" As he asks, Joel's switching on a living room lamp.

"Sinfully sugar-coated peanut butter Christmas cookies … with a chocolate kiss on top?" she adds around a mouthful. "I made a whole tin of them—you know, for my life list. Cook something expertly from scratch. Number seven— done," she manages around more cookie apparently stuffed in her mouth.

"Ah. Another number checked off."

"Yeah, but seriously? Someone needs to take this tin away from me."

There's a quiet pause before Joel answers. "Be right over," he says.

⁂

Faye sits on an old blanket on her front stoop. The night is cold as she waits to spot Joel hurrying across the lawn. When he emerges from the shadows, he has on a navy duffle coat. It hangs loose, the leather toggle buttons not fastened. So she can also see that *beneath* the coat, he still has on his work clothes. But gloves are on his hands; his wool beanie is pulled low.

As he nears, Faye pats the blanketed stoop beside her. So they sit together—their knees bent as they lean close.

In the dark night, then, they talk.

And dig into her cookie tin for a peanut butter blossom or two.

Sitting side by side, their arms press together.

Faye feels the warmth of that closeness.

Their voices are muted. Even.

She admires the tall, illuminated fir tree reaching to the sky in his yard.

He tells her that he hopes she's feeling better.

She huddles beneath her black, cable-knit poncho.

He tells a lame joke.

She laughs. And looks at his scruffy face, his dark eyes.

He takes another cookie from the tin she holds.

They hear a barred owl call in the cold darkness.

*Who-who. Who-whooo.*

Silence, then.

But Joel points in the direction of another owl's answering call.

Faye listens to the sound of the wild. The free.

In the quiet after, Joel reaches an arm around her and gives a brief hug.

He stands, then, too.

Says goodnight.

And takes off with her half-full tin stuffed with peanut butter blossoms.

# twenty-one

By SATURDAY MORNING, THE TAVERN is just about fully decked out. Joel and his staff spent a few hours hanging ornaments and stringing lights on a large flocked Christmas tree near the bar. In the tavern's dark-paneled interior, the tree's white lights glimmer now.

Just in time, too.

The lunch crowd is coming in. A few patrons settle with shopping bags at tables; phoned-in orders are picked up; and Wes Davis sits at the bar. He's in his full mail-carrier uniform and sipping a soda as a waitress takes his order.

Oh, and one more customer arrives. Faye Weston. She walks to her reserved table and slips off her gold-plaid coat. And Joel can see she's gone more formal with today's date. She's dressed all in black—turtleneck sweater to skinny jeans. Black leather ankle boots, and wide gold-buckled black belt. Her hair's different this

162

time around, too. It's pulled back in a short, loose braid. A few strands escape and frame her face.

Once she settles in her chair, Joel walks over with a step stool and the requisite Merry Match candy-cane heart figurine—which he places on her table.

"A lunch date this time?" he asks.

Faye nods. "Thought I'd try a different vibe."

As Joel sets down the step stool, he admits to her that he feels good about this date. "This could be it for you. You know, might be the gem of them all."

"How can you tell?" she asks, eyeing that little stool.

"Well. Third time's the charm?"

"Wait. What are you doing?" she asks when he nudges that stool closer to her table.

From his vest pocket, Joel pulls a small sprig of green leaves and berries. The sprig's tied with a red burlap bow. "Hanging mistletoe around the bar," he says, stepping up on that stool. "This looks like a nice spot."

"*Uh-uh-uh,* Mr. Briggs. One more move and I'm pushing you *off* that stool."

"You sure?" While holding that mistletoe up to a garland swag there, Joel looks down at Faye. At her hazel eyes cautiously watching him. At her short, wispy blonde braid. "It's a good icebreaker, mistletoe," he explains. "You know, it leads to a friendly holiday kiss? I've seen it happen, and you might be surprised." Still his arm holds up that leafy sprig.

"*Joooel.*"

"Okay. But it could be a missed opportunity." He looks over to a couple at a nearby table. "You here on a Merry Match?" he asks them.

"We are!" the woman says.

"Mind if I hang some holiday décor at your table? Your call," he says, holding up the mistletoe sprig.

The man and woman look at each other, shrug ... and then nod. They lean in and kiss, too, once the mistletoe dangles from the garland above them.

And Faye? She just shakes her head with a slight smile as Joel picks up his stool, raises an eyebrow at her and heads back to the bar.

∽

Wes moves his sandwich platter over to the Trouble Tree. His regulation postal service winter coat is unzipped; his trapper hat with faux-fur flaps and postal insignia is on the bar. And he sits quietly there, digging into his buffalo chicken wrap. Occasionally, he also picks up a mini glittered bell ornament from the trouble basket.

"Something on your mind?" Joel asks while grabbing a knife and a few limes.

"Oh, man," Wes says around a mouthful of food. "Got a real pain-in-the-neck trouble in my life."

"Seriously?"

Wes nods and contemplates those glittering trouble ornaments.

"Lay it on me," Joel tells him as he begins slicing the limes.

So Wes does. He first reaches over and loops the thread of a silver glitter bell on a bough of the Trouble Tree. Then he unloads. Talks about the wayward Canada goose living in a patch of woods at the end of Old Willow

Road. And how that goose waddles out of those trees when it hears the mail truck approaching. The feisty fowl then runs alongside the truck and takes little nipping leaps at Wes' hand as he delivers mail to the homes there.

"That bothersome bird's actually pecked me a time or two," Wes says, holding up his hand.

"Maybe give him something to eat, guy," Joel advises. "A piece of bread or something, you know, to calm the bird down."

And as Wes goes on about that being a good idea, and asking Joel if he can spare some bread to take on his route now, Joel's doing something else. While slicing those limes for drinks, he's keeping an ear tuned to Faye's table talk.

Or—should he say—her *date's* table talk. Because the guy's firing off his questions, nonstop. Still, between Wes' trouble-griping, Joel catches a few of Faye's answers. Catches that she's more an early bird than a night owl. That she's lived in Addison all her life. That she doesn't like to travel too far from home—unless for a special reason. That January's her favorite month.

"The *hush* of it. The quiet," she elaborates. "And the hope of it, too."

"What do you like to do in your free time?" her date asks next.

Faye pauses. And glances Joel's way; he sees that. "Free time?" she repeats to her date then. "I play it by ear."

Joel likes that answer. He likes the easiness of it. The respecting the moment.

Faye must like whatever *she's* hearing, too. Because whenever Joel sends a glance *her* way, she's smiling. With

165

every answer, with every question she asks, with every nod as she listens to her date's answers—her smile doesn't fade.

*So …* Joel thinks, slicing his final lime on a small plate. *Maybe this is it. Her gem.*

⤜⤏

Or maybe not.

A half hour later, after Faye's date leaves, she wanders over to the Trouble Tree.

"I have a mouth-ache from fake smiling," she says, then rubs her jaw.

"What?"

"My jaw's a little sore." She looks back to the doorway, then to Joel. "These dates are *exhausting*. I'm constantly nodding and smiling. You know, to be polite. And … open."

"But, well," Joel says, glancing to the door, too. No date is in sight. "How'd it actually go, Faye?"

"It was … *pretty* good, I guess. He's a nice enough guy. And it wasn't really a *blind* date because I already knew him."

"You did?"

Faye nods and toys with a blue glitter bell from the trouble basket. "We went to high school together. He was a year behind me."

"No kidding." Joel rings out a bar tab for a waitress, then turns back to Faye. "But you got along? The date had potential?"

"I have to think about it." Sitting there in her gold-plaid coat, Faye gives her barstool a slow spin and eyes her now-empty date table. "He was kind of … boring.

166

And he mentioned having a lot of student-loan debt. Which I really don't want to know about. Seems like he was saddled with it."

"Come on. We're just talking about going on a date or two," Joel counters, folding back a white shirtsleeve. "Not a lifelong commitment."

"I'm looking ahead, I guess." Faye lifts that blue glittered bell, touches one bough, then another, on the Trouble Tree. Finally, she delicately hangs the tiny ornament. "We'll just see how date number four goes," she quietly says.

## twenty-two

J OEL'S LOOKING AHEAD, TOO.

The tavern was busy all day Saturday. *And* Sunday. Between several scheduled Christmas parties, not to mention hosting more Merry Match dates, he'd put in full days. Then he heard the forecast Sunday evening. A forecast predicting snow later in the week.

So he takes Monday off from work. There's one last pile of rocks that needs stacking on his stone wall. And Monday morning, he's hard at it. Dressed in jeans, a flannel, his down vest, work gloves and a wool hat, he gets the job done.

One heavy stone at a time.

One cracking thud at a time as he sets each stone in place.

One long breath at a time as he two-handedly lifts the next fieldstone.

And the next.

All morning.

He gets that last rock pile dwindling beneath a cloudy December sky.

When his mail's delivered, though, he takes a break from the rock-stacking and walks to his mailbox at the curb. A handful of envelopes are there, so he brings them inside—wanting to warm up, too.

By the time he's gotten to his front door, he's thumbing through the envelopes.

And by the time he's in his kitchen, he sees a Christmas card from Faye.

It's the one piece of mail he holds after setting the rest on the counter. He looks at the ornate handwriting on her envelope. Taps the sealed envelope in his palm. Sits at his kitchen table and glances outside in the direction of her little peaked bungalow.

And opens the envelope.

Oh, Joel totally *gets* the card's snowy image of a country home nestled in the trees. The house is aglow; snow falls from an evening sky. It's all Faye. She loves nothing more than her *own* country house.

But the charm doesn't come from the image.

Joel's actually charmed by something else as he sits there in his flannel shirt and jeans and work boots and puffy vest and wool hat—all still on.

He's charmed when he opens the actual card and sees the message Faye penned. The ornate letters slope and curve and loop in harmony.

It has him smile, that message, as he reads it once more.

*Note the fancy penmanship! I've been taking calligraphy lessons and checked off Number 4 on my life list—learn a new art form.*

*Happy holidays, my friend!*

First, Joel glances out his window again.

Then, before getting back to his rock wall, he takes that card to his living room.

Looks around.

Crosses the room.

And stands the card, carefully, beside a carved wooden deer atop his fireplace mantel.

❧

Late Monday morning, Faye's standing on Joel's front porch and ringing his doorbell. She holds a Christmas card, too. It's one of those personalized postcards made with a photograph of the sender, or the sender's family. While waiting at Joel's door, she looks at the picture of a smiling woman with a golden retriever. They're both wearing matching Santa hats and sitting together beside a decorated Christmas tree. Beneath the picture, the custom imprinted message reads, *Merry Christmas from Denise and Duke.* But Faye's eyes go, again, to the *handwritten* message scrawled there, too.

*Miss you, Joel. Will be in town visiting a friend. Dinner?*

The thing is? Faye's surprised to feel her heart drop with that message. To feel a … chance, maybe … slip away.

*"What?"* she whispers, tapping that Christmas postcard

on her open hand. Shaking her head then, she brushes aside some startling twinge of sadness. And tugs her coat closed against the cold. There's no answer at Joel's door, but his pickup truck is in the driveway. So she wanders around to his side yard and spots him at his rock wall.

"Hey, neighbor," she calls out, heading in his direction.

"Faye." Joel finishes up with a rock he'd lifted, then takes off his work gloves. "What's up?"

"I just stopped home after a dentist appointment, and I'm on my way to work now," she explains once she gets to that rambling stone wall. "But I checked my mail, and ..." She pauses and looks at the Christmas postcard, then at Joel. "I thought this was a magazine subscription notice at first, but it's not. It's for you, actually. And I was just going to put it in your mailbox, but saw you were around."

"Yeah, I took the day off to finish up my rock wall." Joel glances to the sky. "Snow's predicted later in the week. And hey, thanks for *your* card. That calligraphy was really something. Nice job, Weston."

"Glad you liked it." Faye holds out that photo-postcard now. "And here's *another* holiday card for you. One with a Christmas dinner-date invite," she says, her voice slightly catching.

"What?" Joel takes the card and gives it a skim.

"I couldn't help but see," Faye's explaining. "It's a postcard from a pretty lady and her dog." As Joel reads the penned message scrawled across the bottom of the picture, Faye pulls her keys from her coat pocket and backs away. "So ... let me know how *your* date goes!"

Joel gives a distracted wave as she turns toward her driveway.

171

While crossing his yard, though, Faye looks back at Joel. Just once. When she does, he's looking up from the postcard and their eyes briefly meet.

"Done. If the rock wall needs any adjustments, we'll get them in the spring," Joel tells his brother later that afternoon. "Thanks for your help, though."

"No prob. I had to stay away from my house, you know? It's being overtaken by Brooke and her sister and their wedding prep. Even the baby seems into it." Brett sits at the firepit near the rock wall. He's got on earmuffs and a down jacket—which he huddles into. The fire crackles in the fading sunlight. A few hot dogs roast over the flames. He grabs a cold beer from Joel, too. "So I'm glad you took the day off," Brett says, snapping open his beer can and taking a swig. "Gave me somewhere to go after work."

"Couldn't have finished the wall without you." Joel sits in a chair near his custom stone firepit. He takes the long handles of the roasting forks and gives the food a turn over the fire.

"*Ahh.*" Brett leans back in his chair. "This sure beats finalizing a seating chart. Brooke and Vera have the reception hall all mapped out and are at the kitchen table moving around guest names there." Brett sits up then and leans to the fire. "You really not bringing a date to the wedding, bro?"

"I'd like to," Joel says. "But it's not in the cards, man." Leaning his arms on his knees, he turns the hot dogs

172

again. "I'll tell you. December's a month that sneaks up on me. Messes with me a little, too."

"How so?"

Joel reaches for his own beer now. "It's just that, the rest of the year? I'm swamped. I'm busy with the tavern. The house, yard work. Family things. Bingo nights. And I'm feeling good, you know? Never better." He takes a swig of beer before setting the can down and looking over at his brother. "But December kind of takes me by the shoulders and gives a shake. You know, it makes me realize twelve months have gone by. And ..." In the shadows of the flickering fire, Joel just turns up his hands.

"And you didn't find someone," Brett finishes.

"No. Not this year."

"But you meet people all the time at work."

"The tavern's not that kind of place. It's more locals and couples, friends and families. People celebrating milestones, watching the games. It's a gathering place, not a pickup joint. And anyway, I'm out of there by five most nights."

"Yeah," Brett says, turning up the collar of his down jacket. "It's tough. I mean, if Brooke hadn't come in to get her taxes done back in the day? Not sure I would've met someone, either."

Joel stands then. Adjusts the wool beanie he wears. He walks to the stone wall, too, and gives a rock a nudge before turning back to the firepit. The flames throw wavering shadows. The sky's deep lavender at sunset. "I got a Christmas card from Denise today. Out of the blue," he says, sitting in his fireside chair again.

"No kidding."

173

"Yeah. She's going to be in town and asked about having dinner together."

"Huh. It didn't work out with you two the first time, Joel. Think dinner's a good idea?"

"Don't know." Joel lifts the hot dogs off the fire and arranges them on a large plate. "Maybe I should've gone to Saratoga Springs with Denise, after all," he's saying while pulling hot dog buns from a bag. "Started a life together there. Because ... was Denise it for me? The best it could be?"

"Everything would've been different, though."

"What do you mean?"

"Dad's tavern would've been sold. You wouldn't be around ..."

Joel gives a nod.

"Who knows, man?" Brett stands and walks around the firepit to the food. "Making decisions sucks sometimes."

"Tell me about it."

"So anyway, toss me a bun, would you?"

"*Eh.*" Joel takes a bun and throws it at his brother. "Heads up, bro. It's cold out here, let's get these toasted and take the food inside."

# twenty-three

EARLY TUESDAY EVENING, JOEL'S BUFFING the tavern's six-panel black door. Through the door's sidelights, he sees tiny flakes swirl in the glow of colonial lampposts outside. He also sees Faye hurrying along the cobblestone walkway, so he opens the door for her.

"Hey, Faye," he says, stepping aside as she blusters in from the cold.

"Here we go again!" she tells him, brushing snow off her coat sleeves. "Your entertainment for the hour."

"Oh, come on." Joel crosses his arms as she heads to her nearby table. "It's not like that."

As Faye takes off that gold-plaid coat, she looks over at him. "I'm officially giving up on these Merry Match dates after tonight."

"What number is this one?"

"Mystery man number four."

"Then you're out the door?"

"Well, I'll tell you." Faye pauses to hang her coat on her chairback. "I can't take much more of this."

Joel watches as she fusses at the table. Faye's all in beige this time—beige fisherman sweater over fitted beige jeans. A thick knitted beige scarf is looped around her neck. He notices other things, too, like her brushed-gold ball earrings when she tucks back her blonde hair. And how her face is flushed from the snowy, cold weather outside.

Until he realizes he's maybe noticing too much.

So they make small talk, then. She asks if he's getting the door ready for the tavern's New Year's shindig.

"Yeah," he says, taking his rag and giving the door a final swipe. "My father's dropping off another basket of mini corn brooms tonight." Joel shoves that rag in his back pocket and glances out again through the sidelights—for his dad, this time. "Just a couple more weeks till we sweep out the old again."

Faye pulls out the chair at her table and sits. "And in with the new," she answers, while keeping an eye on the door.

"Hey, Weston. Maybe number four is the new for *you*," Joel tells her on his way back to the bar. But in no time, he's at her date table again. After setting down the candy-cane heart figurine, he gives her a folded *Addison Weekly*. It's open to the *Shop Local* section. "And nice work here," he says, pointing to the feature photograph of a holiday dining room. The planked wood table is finely set. Dinner plates are arranged on a long plaid runner strewn with balsam boughs. Snow-dusted pinecones and glimmering fat red candles on silver pedestals dot those green fir twigs. Bottlebrush trees nestled in cottony faux snow make up the centerpiece. And the glimmering silver flatware is all Silver Settings'.

"Oh, thanks, Joel." She turns the paper to better see. "My staff worked *so* hard on that photo shoot."

"And *I* right away recognized the peanut butter blossoms on that cookie platter," Joel adds with an easy wink.

Faye smiles—but is suddenly distracted by a man coming into the tavern, pausing and looking around.

Joel looks over, too, then back to Faye. "It's go time," he quietly says, then gives her a nod, scoops up the paper and walks back to the bar.

Faye stands. The man in the doorway wears a gray wool coat over a black-and-gray striped sweater and black pants. "Luca?" she asks.

"Yes," he says, walking toward her and extending his hand. "Luca Leone, very pleased to meet you."

"Faye Weston. And likewise!" When she shakes his hand, he double clasps hers. They do a little awkward stepping back to the table, too—he moving this way, she moving that—until finally Luca pulls out the chair for her.

But that's as awkward as they get. Once Luca sits and pulls his chair slightly closer, it's like they're old friends. He just has a way about him she finds so ... *easy.*

Okay, they hit it off.

Right away, she's taken by his animated manner, his wavy dark hair, his close beard. His smile as he explains how he's been so busy at his family's pizzeria.

"Luigi's?" Faye interrupts.

"That's the one."

"Nice place."

"It is. But I haven't had time to put myself *out there* since coming back to the family business. Still—I love this town and figure it can't hurt to meet others who feel the same. So … Merry Match seemed like a great way to do that."

And that's how they talk—in long sentences like they just can't get enough, or say enough, to the other. They lean close. And laugh. And pause only to give the waitress their drink order.

And that's just in the first five minutes.

Once they settle in and their drinks are delivered, Luca lifts a bag he'd brought and pulls out a single-slice pizza box. He slides it across their table.

"What is this?" Faye asks.

He shrugs. "Some people bring a flower. A corsage, maybe. And I bring pizza. A deluxe pizza slice—just for you."

"That is *so* nice, Luca. *And* thoughtful."

Luca nods. "Have it later on. Pizza always tastes better late at night. And … I hope you'll eventually give me a call and let me know how you liked it."

"At this number?" Faye points to the number printed on the box.

"That's the restaurant number, but I'll give you my cell. Do you have a pen?" When Faye hands him one from her purse, he scrawls his personal phone number on the box. When he's done, he also taps a line of block writing on the box that reads: *HOT AND DELICIOUS. PLEASE CALL*

*AGAIN.* "Now … whether that line refers to the pizza, *or* to yours truly—I'll leave to you."

Again, Faye laughs. Easily and genuinely.

⁓◯

Joel's back to work. And busy. The blustering snow flurry drives in the customers. So he mixes drinks, pulls drafts, wipes down the bar, rings out tabs.

And keeps an eye and ear on one particular date table. As he does, he can't help thinking of what he told Faye at the Trouble Tree after her first dud of a date. *Give it a chance. There'll be some gem in there. You'll see.*

And there he is—the gem. Luca Leone.

It's obvious this Luca and Faye are a real … match. A *legit* Merry Match.

Because as they toss questions back and forth, and go off on tangents, there's no missing that Faye's smitten. Luca is, too. They lean close. She clasps his arm when she's talking. They watch only each other. There are no uncomfortable pauses. Only a bona fide connection, especially as they ask a few rapid-fire questions. Joel doesn't hear them all over the noise, but he hears enough.

> From Luca: *Three words to describe yourself.*
> From Faye: *Right now? Relieved. Happy. Surprised. You?*
> From Luca: *The very same! Favorite place to go?*
> From Faye: *Home! At the end of a workday. Just … home. I love it there.*
> From Luca: *That's nice, Faye. And a rarity.*
> From Faye: *What about you? Your favorite place to go?*

179

At first, Joel notices, Luca doesn't answer. He just stands, holds out his hand and nods to The Green outside. "Favorite place to go?" he repeats. "Tonight? The town Christmas tree. Join me?"

There's a flurry of motion, then, as Faye stands and Luca helps her on with her coat.

As Luca takes out his wallet and covers the tab, leaving the money on the table.

As they walk across the planked hardwood floor and leave together, arms looped.

As they push through the six-panel black tavern door and head out in the light snow.

With no glance back from Faye.

No wave. No return to the Trouble Tree in the next hour or so.

Nothing.

So Joel tells Kevin he's going into his office for a while. When he's in there, he shuts the door, then gives it a swift kick when it doesn't catch. He also turns on one lamp, looks around and sinks into his big old desk chair.

Slams closed a partially open desk drawer.

And flops back in that chair.

Draws his hands over his eyes, too, whispering, *"Damn it."*

When there's a knock at his office door, he calls out, "Busy! Not a good time."

But the knock comes again.

So Joel leans forward, elbows on his desk and calls again, "I said—later!"

Still, the door slowly opens until Joel sees his father poke his head in.

"Joel?" he asks. "It's just me. I have the latest batch of whisk brooms. A few wing-styles in this bunch. They're all dyed, too. Reds, greens." His father, wearing a thin cardigan over a button-down and corduroy pants, ventures slowly into the office. Tufts of gray hair show from beneath his wool cap. His jacket is slung across the broom basket. And his caution is obvious as he sets down that loaded basket. "You know, it's getting *awfully* close to New Year's. You'll be needing these."

"Okay, sorry," Joel tells him from the shadows. "You can leave them there."

There's a quiet moment before his father talks. "What's the matter with you?"

Joel sits back in his desk chair. Blows out a breath, too. "I'm going to lose her."

"What? Lose who?"

Joel's voice comes low now. Low and even. "Lose the woman I'm in love with who doesn't even know it."

His father tips his head and walks closer. "You sound really serious, Joel."

"I am serious." Joel drags a hand back through his hair. "And I'm also too late."

His father looks at him, then gently closes the office door, pulls a straight chair up to the desk and sits there. "Come on," he tells Joel. "Let's talk."

181

# twenty-four

"HOW WOULD YOU DESCRIBE THIS pizza?" Faye asks while cutting Luca's pizza slice neatly in half. She puts one piece on Sadie's dish. It's late Wednesday afternoon, and they're sitting at Faye's white-painted kitchen table. The lacy drum-shade chandelier drops soft light on the table; the windowpane mirror leaning atop the mantel is nestled now in a balsam garland. Brushed-gold ornaments glimmer in that garland. Tiny white lights strung through it twinkle as she and Sadie have supper.

And when Sadie lifts her pizza slice, Faye reminds her, "I need adjectives. *Good* ones."

So Sadie digs in. She cups that large piece of pizza that Faye reheated and takes a double bite of the cheesy, saucy slice. "Mouthwatering," Sadie says around the food. "Amazing, too." She closes her eyes with another bite and murmurs, eyes still closed, *"Tender."*

Well. Faye has to see for herself. Or taste for herself.

So after doling out a salad, and spooning scoopfuls of homemade macaroni and cheese onto their plates, and pouring some wine, she does it. She takes a big bite of that pizza slice—and can only moan. With pleasure.

"I know. Sinful isn't it?" Sadie asks, her voice almost a whisper.

Faye smiles. "It's that good."

"Must've been one *heck* of a date."

"You saved the best for last."

"Details, please," Sadie says, then takes another bite of that magical pizza.

"I don't have many," Faye tells her, sipping her wine now. "Luca had to get back to work. His family's pizza place was busy and they needed him at the ovens." She lifts a forkful of macaroni and cheese. "But he's very charming. And easy to be with."

Sadie nods and tells her she's glad. That's what she'd hoped would come from her Merry Match dates. As they eat, Faye fills in more details. She tells Sadie how she and Luca took a walk around The Green. And lingered near the town Christmas tree before he headed back to Luigi's.

"Well, you mentioned you're going to Vera's wedding Saturday," Sadie says later when she brings dishes to the kitchen sink. "Could you invite Luca?"

"Oh, no." Faye's rinsing their dishes and loading the dishwasher. "It's too soon. I don't really know him enough for that."

"What do you mean?" As she asks, Sadie takes a wet dishrag and wipes off the kitchen island.

"It's just that ... when you go to a wedding with a *date*, you look at each other and envision *yourselves* at the altar.

And that's a little too much after only *one* date." Faye closes the dishwasher, then turns to Sadie. "But Luca and I plan to get together again after the holidays. Everyone's super busy right now. You know how it is ... so close to Christmas."

"Do I ever." Sadie heads to the hallway coat closet for her parka. First, though, she picks up a slim, pale-gray pitcher from an accent table there. "This is nice," she remarks, brushing her fingers across the finish. "Is it new?"

"Oh, that. Yeah." Faye joins her in the front hallway. "Joel picked that out."

"Joel?"

"Mm-hmm. At the Merry Market. We were doing some Christmas shopping."

"You? And ... *Joel?*" Sadie asks, raising a curious eyebrow, pitcher still in hand.

"Yes." Faye pulls Sadie's black parka from the closet. "And it's not what you think."

"But ... could it be?"

"What? Joel? I mean, yes, he's a really nice guy."

"Easy on the eyes, too," Sadie adds, setting the pitcher back on the table.

Faye gives a light laugh. "He is. *And* he's my neighbor, Sadie. So we're friends, that's all."

"Well, stranger things have happened," Sadie suggests, taking her parka from Faye. "And *I'm* off to meet Harry now. We're going to see his nephew, Oliver, sing at his school Christmas concert," she says, slipping her arms into the jacket sleeves. "What are you up to tonight?"

Faye walks her to the door while telling her she'll be doing some sewing. "It's on my life list, no less! Number twelve:

Learn to sew a button. I looked online for instructions," she adds, flashing her cell phone screen to Sadie.

And wastes no time tackling that number twelve. Once she waves off Sadie, Faye settles on a big tufted club chair in her living room. A table lamp shines close by as she pulls a gray knitted throw off the back of the chair and drapes it over her lap.

She's ready to begin.

So she lifts her cute fabric sewing basket off the antique-trunk coffee table. Next, she brushes through her meticulously aligned sewing notions. There's a pincushion, and hand needles, and a thimble, and tape measure. Finally, she gets to the mini spools of thread all in a row. Brown. Green. Blue. Pink. White. Red.

"Oh, no." Faye lifts the sewing basket's top tray and looks beneath that. She moves aside scissors and a seam puller. "*Gah!* No black thread?" Her beautiful black velvet dress with the loose button is draped over the arm of her club chair.

Her dress for Derek and Vera's winter wedding—three days away.

Faye sets aside her sewing basket and, in a panic, runs to her kitchen window. She squints out into the darkness, looks across the yard and sees Joel's house next door. His tall fir tree out front is all lit up. Lights are on in his windows, too. So she grabs her cell phone and sends a quick text message.

❦

A few pull-chain bulbs cast dim light in the attic. Joel's careful as he walks through the shadowed space. Old wooden rafters crisscross above him. Boxes and dusty furniture are stacked here and there. He opens an old metal-banded leather trunk filled with blankets. Closes that and opens the flaps of a big carton—right as his cell phone dings. He pulls it from his back pocket and squints in the low light to read a text message from Faye.

*Do you happen to have any black thread?*

Sitting on that leather trunk now, he thumb-types back. *Have to check. What for?*

*35 Things Before 35 List. No. 12: Learn to sew a button. Have a really loose one that needs fixing.*

Joel shakes his head with an easy smile. *In the attic getting XM decoration*, he types. *Come by.* He maneuvers himself and the necessary box in his arms down the attic stairs then. Once in the living room, he lifts a large vintage ceramic Christmas tree from that cardboard carton. The tree's wrapped in wads of old newspaper to keep it from chipping in storage. So after peeling away the paper, he sets the tree on a wide ledge in a side window. Just then, there's a knock at his front door.

"It's open," he yells while centering that ceramic tree.

Seconds later, Faye comes in all a-fluster. Her gold-plaid wool coat hangs open over some tunic sweater and black leggings and her shearling-lined suede ankle boots. Already she's saying how this is such a big help, him having black thread, and mentions how cold it is outside, and that she might've just heard one of the barred owls off in the trees.

But she stops still when he plugs in that green ceramic tree in his window. The tips of the green boughs are frosted white. Tiny bulbs of red, yellow and green light up on the tree.

186

*"Oh, nice,"* Faye says, obviously taken with the sight.

Joel steps back and looks from the tree, to her. To her blonde hair mussed from the cold wind outside. To her hazel eyes locked on that tree—until she looks at him.

"I've always loved those ceramic trees." She walks closer and gently touches one of the shining bulbs. "There's something *so* nostalgic about them." Standing there, she brushes some dust off the ceramic boughs, then moves the tree—slightly—to the left. "I'll go outside to be sure it's centered."

Before he can stop her—before he's said *anything,* actually—she's out the door. A muffled silence falls over the room in her sudden absence. Until there's a rap on the window. When Joel looks, she gives a thumbs-up before hurrying back inside.

"Come on in the kitchen," he tells her. "It's where I'd have any thread lying around."

"Oh, I really hope you do."

Faye follows behind him, stopping in the kitchen doorway when he opens a drawer there filled with menus, stray keys, scissors—and random spools of thread.

He looks over his shoulder at her. "Something need repairing?"

Faye nods. "A dress. A button is really loose on my black velvet dress."

"Velvet?" he asks, rifling through the drawer. "Going on a swanky date?"

"Ha! No. To a wedding."

Joel stops rifling and turns to her again. "Derek and Vera's?"

"Yes! Hey, aren't you going, too?"

"I am. My brother is married to Vera's sister. So it's all kind of family."

"Right, right. You mentioned that." Faye leans against the kitchen doorjamb now. "Silver Settings is providing the flatware for their reception. We work with the boathouse for special occasions like that. And after all my consultations with Vera? She invited me to the wedding, sort of last minute."

Holding a dusty spool of black thread, Joel leans against the kitchen counter and crosses his arms. "You bringing someone?" he asks.

Faye shakes her head, no. "How about you? Bringing ... Denise, maybe?"

He silently shakes his head, too. And just watches her for a second.

"Well." Faye takes a quick breath. "I guess I'll see you there!"

"Yeah." He steps forward and gives her the black thread. "Or ... we can just go together. You know—as friends."

"Really? I'd like that." She tips her head with an unexpected smile. "You sure?"

"I'll pick you up."

When she nods, and after they agree on a time, he walks her out the front door. And as she crosses the lawn to her house, Joel stands on his front porch and watches her in the shadows. And waves when she looks back at him. He also thinks of what his father said last night in the tavern office—when Joel told him he actually fell in love with the girl next door.

Thinks of how his father said, *You have to give it a shot, Joel. Give it your best and you won't regret it.*

188

Joel looks once more as Faye gets to her bungalow's entry alcove.

And his father's words ring in his mind.

*The only thing you'll ever regret ... is not trying.*

# twenty-five

THE PANELING IN FAYE'S BEDROOM is painted a pale gray. A white down-filled comforter covers her bed. Thin brushed-steel table lamps topped with white fabric drum shades sit on each of the white country-style end tables. The lamps throw a soft light on the room. Dark hardwood floors gleam. The dormered ceiling slants on one wall; a large, gold club chair is draped with a fringed gray-and-white windowpane throw; the old silver radiator ticks with rising heat.

*Hipstoric*, Faye thinks while standing there late Saturday afternoon. Old and new blended throughout.

"And classic," she says aloud, lifting a black velvet sheath off the bed. She steps into the dress, slips her arms in the long, narrow sleeves and shimmies the fitted fabric into place on her chest, her hips, her legs. Twisting around, she manages to zip up the back—leaving undone the three top buttons—which are just out of reach of her fingers.

But all the while, as she gets ready for Vera and Derek's wedding, there's something more.

As she next clips her hair in a loose chignon, and puts on pearl chandelier earrings, and a narrow gold watch, and slips into her black high-heeled ankle booties—yes, there's *something*. In her heart, maybe. Or her breathing. Her spine, and her shoulders, give a shiver.

In the bathroom now, she leans over the sink to the mirror and applies her makeup. Mascara. Light blush. Red lipstick. Which is when it happens—right when she holds the lipstick to her mouth.

Her hand slightly shakes, too.

So she pauses and takes a breath—then manages to finish her lips.

And notices she's actually smiling. Just a little. But it's like, well, it's like she's got *butterflies* or something.

Which has her study her reflection before dropping the lipstick and a comb into her gold envelope clutch. Back in her bedroom, she gives her full reflection a final once-over—pressing the fabric of her velvet sheath here, there. Turning some and glancing at her side view, too.

⁓

Suddenly, it's Saturday.

And suddenly, it's time.

Time to pick up Faye.

So Joel buttons a navy suit vest over his denim shirt and navy suit pants. Ties his oxford shoes. Checks his hair and face in the bedroom mirror. He hasn't shaved in a few days, so there's a shadow of whiskers on his jaw. He drags a hand through his dark hair, puts on his suede rust-colored field jacket, lifts the collar and heads out to his pickup truck.

Minutes later, he's next door and on Faye's walkway. Light snow coats it, making his leather shoes slip and slide some. Ahead, his *Welcome* sign stands in the bungalow's entry alcove. Twinkling white lights are strung around the barnboard sign now. There's a big balsam wreath hanging on Faye's door, too. Joel stands there in the shadowed alcove, tugs his jacket sleeves and clears his throat before ringing the doorbell.

When the door sweeps open, lamplight spills outside. Faye's there, too, a silhouette against that light.

"Hey, Joel! Come in, come in." She motions him inside. "I'll just be a minute."

And suddenly, Joel's stopped just inside her door as Faye steps back. She wears a fitted, long-sleeve black velvet dress, sheer black stockings and high-heeled ankle boots. Her blonde hair is twisted back, leaving wispy bangs sweeping over her eyes and alongside her pretty face. Pearl-and-gold earrings dangle; a gold chain falls into the deep V neckline of that velvet dress. A wool camel coat drapes over an arm.

And it takes Joel a few long seconds to realize he needs to talk.

"You look *beautiful*, Faye." He gives a small shake of his head. "You *really* do."

"You're too kind, Joel. And hey, look at *you*, Mr. Handsome."

"Eh," he says, waving her off, then glancing out the door behind him. "Listen, it's snowing a little. You'll need that coat on."

"I know. But ..." She pauses as she turns her back to him. "Would you mind buttoning my dress first? There are three buttons," she says over her shoulder. "I tried, but they were tricky to reach."

Joel hesitates, then steps closer as she's waiting—her back to him, her head tipped down. Very gently, he starts with the lowest button. It's black velvet, too. His fingers brush Faye's skin as he works that tiny button and maneuvers the smooth velvet of the dress. When he moves to the second one, he asks, "This where you sewed on a button?"

Faye nods. A few wisps of hair have fallen from her chignon. They sweep along the soft skin of her neck. "The top one," her quiet voice says. "How'd I do?"

Joel, standing close, sees her tipped face as she talks. He moves his fingers to that newly sewn button and carefully presses it through the buttonhole. "Fastens like a charm," he tells her, giving the velvet dress a light pat and stepping back.

And he sees it, the way her eyes drop closed for a long second.

*"Okay,"* Faye whispers, turning back to him now. An awkward pause comes when she looks at him—but says nothing else.

So he reaches for that coat on her arm. "Here. Let me help you with that."

Once more, she turns.

And suddenly, they stand close again.

Suddenly, he's lifting her coat and guiding one velvet-clad arm into a sleeve, then the other arm.

Suddenly, he's behind her and adjusting the camel wool

coat on her shoulders, then turning her to him. Her smile is slight, but warm, as he straightens and tugs the lapels of her coat close. "You're all set, Faye," he says then.

She silently watches him, just long enough for him to notice, before clearing her throat and reaching for her clutch from a nearby table.

And suddenly again—just like that—they're out the door and into the cold, snowy evening.

# *twenty-six*

THE OLD BARN AT THE cove takes their breath away.

As they walk in, a lone piano plays a soft melody. Candles flicker in every paned window. Hundreds of delicate gold snowflake ornaments hang from the barn's rough-hewn rafters. Those snowflakes catch the glimmering candlelight and reflect a pale hue on the rustic barn's dark interior. Vera had partially cleared the main floor of her Christmas shoppe, Snowflakes and Coffee Cakes, and all her wedding guests now sit on chairs arranged there.

Inside the barn, simple white lights also shine from a few clustered trees. Those tiny lights cast a faint glow around them—so there's actually a solemn air to the setting. Lush balsam boughs are strung along the loft railing, too. More white lights twinkle in those fresh greens.

And now, all eyes are on Vera and Derek. They stand with the officiant beneath the loft area. Vera's fitted gown is cream-colored with a small train. A sheer shawl wraps around her shoulders; long cream gloves reach to her elbows. Derek stands beside her in a black tuxedo.

"Before we begin," the officiant announces, "if I can direct your attention to the side wall, please."

There's a hum of voices and motion as the guests all turn while whispering questions. Joel sees his brother, Brett—who is Derek's best man—standing at the side wall. Double barn doors there are accented with crossbeams. Brett takes the wrought-iron door handles and slowly opens those double doors—one at a time. When he does, gasps and murmurs rise at the sight of an expansive evening view of the cove outside. The twilight horizon is silver with snow clouds. Dark blue cove waters are still.

But there's more.

Outdoor spotlights capture tall snow-dusted cove grasses of pale brown topped with silver feathery seed. The dry grasses sway in the cold breeze, almost like a whisper. A towering fresh-cut balsam fir stands just outside the barn doors, too. That tree is also strung with white lights, but looks nearly silver beneath threads of tinsel draped from every branch.

What silences the guests, though, is beyond.

Is anchored in the cove.

It's a lone rowboat with a small Christmas tree in it. That tree also shines with only white lights. The whole outdoor scene—from the sweeping cove grasses to the gentle snow falling on the lone, floating boat—looks almost like an altar itself.

To Derek, Joel's sure it is. It's a place Derek must visit; a place where he might bow his head in reverence to his daughter. The daughter he tragically lost to those waters eleven years ago now. It was a dark December day when little Abby Cooper drowned after falling through the ice.

And Joel knows.

Tonight, the view is *not* heartbreaking. It's not sad.

Faye leans close, clasps Joel's arm and whispers, *"Oh, Joel."*

Joel nods and whispers back, *"They're letting in Abigail's spirit. Derek's daughter."*

*"It's just beautiful,"* Faye answers, her eyes riveted to the scene outside the barn's side doors.

When Brett returns to his place behind Derek, the wedding ceremony commences. Derek and Vera say their personal vows in the candlelit barn. Shadows waver on the dark walls; golden light glimmers. And all the while, Derek and Vera's voices rise, filling the cavernous space with hope and peace and love.

∽◯

At the reception afterward, all Joel sees is silver and white.

The Addison Boathouse is edged with twinkling lights looking silver against the gray December clouds—clouds dropping swirling white snowflakes to the ground. And beyond the boathouse, the winding ribbon of the Connecticut River glimmers silver, too.

He and Faye walk into the reception hall together—where it's more of the same.

"This is just incredible," Faye tells him when they stop in the arched doorway.

Joel takes it all in. The boathouse windows and

observation deck are all lined with more white lights. White lights are strung through swags of green garland looped across the reception room's vaulted, beamed ceiling. And a tall Christmas tree—bedecked in only white lights—anchors the center of the room. White linens drape over the tables; white-and-silver pendant lights hang from the white rafters.

Even more noticeable is the sea of motion. Guests stream in. Everyone was so moved by the barn ceremony, they all want to cut loose and celebrate now. As Joel and Faye look for their table, couples brush past. Brett and his wife say hello on their way to the head table. Harry and Sadie, too. Everyone's smiling. Everyone's happy to see Derek and Vera married.

After leaving her camel coat and his suede field jacket at the coat check, Faye takes Joel's arm and walks beside him in the crowded space. He feels her pressed close.

"The flatware looks amazing," Joel tells her, nodding to the tables. Each silver place setting includes a sprig of white baby's breath—all tied with a string of twine. Candles flickering in hurricane-lantern centerpieces drop soft light on the entwined forks, knives and spoons. A mini magnifier is set out beside each place setting, too.

"I was here yesterday with my staff to get it all set up," Faye tells him as he spots their table number.

Another couple he doesn't recognize is already seated. They're dressed to the nines—he in a black suit, she in a dark-green sequined cocktail dress. Joel pulls out Faye's chair before sitting himself. And he can't help but look once, then again, at Faye beside him. At the way her blonde hair shimmers in the candlelight; at how glad she seems to be here; at how elegant her black velvet dress looks. He puts an arm around her shoulder for a moment, too. That velvet dress is soft beneath his touch as he pulls her close. "Okay, I'm saying it again. You look stunning, Weston," he murmurs into her hair.

Faye glances at him with a smile and gives his hand on her shoulder a squeeze.

Just then, the other man at the table picks up a mini magnifying glass. "Have any idea what these are for?" he asks Joel.

"Sure do." Joel picks one up and demonstrates. "They're meant to be kept in your coat pocket so that when it snows," he says, holding his magnifier over his own arm, "you can look at the snowflakes up close."

"Or as Vera puts it," Faye adds, "they're to really *see* when some wonder drops into your life."

"How do you like that?" The man across from him slips his magnifier into his suit pocket. "I'm Jason, by the way. Jason Barlow." He reaches across the table to shake Joel's hand. "This is my wife, Maris."

"Joel Briggs," Joel says, reaching over and shaking both of their hands. "And Faye Weston. Friends of the newlyweds."

"Nice to meet you," Faye tells them both.

They're interrupted when the band starts and the singer announces the bride and groom's first dance. A slow song begins, the lights drop low and the lone couple sweeps onto the dance floor.

"I grew up in Addison," this Maris says after briefly watching the couple dance. She leans into Jason as she talks. "On Birch Lane."

"Ah, I know the street well," Joel remarks.

Maris nods. "Vera, Brooke and I go way back. Ran into each other during our summers at Stony Point, too."

"Vera and Derek actually came to our seaside wedding two years ago," Jason goes on, sipping from a glass of water. "Derek arranged an illuminated flotilla on Long Island Sound during our reception."

"Sounds fabulous," Faye says, her voice hushed.

"That's Derek for you," Joel agrees. "Top shelf with everything."

"That flotilla made the night all the more special," Maris says.

There's a quiet moment, then, as the four of them watch the newlyweds dance beneath a soft spotlight.

"You two next to get hitched?" Jason asks Joel and Faye—all while motioning to Derek and Vera dancing. "You look well together."

"Us?" Joel looks quickly from Jason, to Faye, then back to Jason. "No. No, just friends."

"*Okay.*" Jason squints over at them with a knowing grin. "Whatever you say."

⁓

*Whatever you say.*

The words stay with Joel. As they talk more with the Barlows during dinner about what they do—Jason, a coastal architect; Maris, a denim-designer-turned-novelist. As Faye mentions she recognizes Jason as host of the public TV show *Castaway Cottage*. And as Faye tells them about the country bungalow she recently bought.

And as Joel talks about the architectural history of his tavern.

Still, the words are there … *Whatever you say.*

As the singer strikes up the band again.

As, instead of joining the others on the dance floor, Faye and Joel head outside to the boathouse observation deck. Alone there, they lean on the expansive white railings. Down below, dark forest edges the Connecticut River. Its winding water flows beneath lightly falling snow. The night is quiet.

In a moment, Joel reaches into his vest pocket. "Come here," he says, motioning Faye closer. "Look."

Faye moves over. "What am I looking at?"

Joel takes her black-velvet-clad arm and gently holds it. Next he lowers that mini magnifier to a few random, sparkling snowflakes alighting on her velvet dress sleeve.

"Oh my goodness," Faye says, tipping her head as she looks. Every sparkling crystal is visible under the magnifier. "They're so … *intricate.* And *beautiful.*"

Their arms press together as they stand above the river and a flurry falls from the night sky. Faye takes the magnifier from him now and holds it over the denim fabric of the cuffed shirt he wears beneath his suit vest. As she wavers it, Joel takes her hand in his and slowly moves it until stopping the magnifier over a large crystal snowflake.

*"Ooh,"* Faye nearly whispers as she leans in to see. "Looks like a star, Joel." She glances at him, her face just inches away as they lean on that railing, as snowflakes drop from the sky. *"A pretty winter star,"* she does whisper, her voice filled with wonder while their eyes meet, so close.

A few seconds pass when there's just the hiss of snowflakes falling on the railing, on Faye's velvet-clad shoulder, on wispy strands of her hair.

A few seconds when they only watch each other.

"Make a wish," Joel tells her, his voice low as he nods to the crystal star on his sleeve.

She doesn't look down at the snowflake, though. The music kicks up a notch behind them in the reception hall. Voices from inside carry out. But Faye, standing so close, looks only at him. And tips her head. *"Joel,"* she whispers.

"Go on. One wish ... before it melts."

Still, she doesn't look at the snowflake.

*Just friends,* he'd insisted earlier at their table.

*Whatever you say,* Jason answered.

With a small smile, Faye finally drops her eyes closed for a long moment.

A quiet, private moment Joel could stay in all night.

A moment after which he and Faye hesitate, then turn to the raucous dancing going down behind them.

"Shall we?" Joel asks, offering his arm to her.

❦

And dance they do.

With each rocking Christmas song the band plays, he and Faye cut loose even more. But when *The Hucklebuck* starts up, the band's singer takes off his suit jacket, grabs his mic and leads the guests. A crowd of people lines the dance floor as Faye and Joel easily fall into step. Everyone's groovin' to this one—Harry and Sadie, kicking right; Brett and Brooke, kicking left; Derek and

Vera, jumping into a turn. Even Jason Barlow and his wife, Maris, get in on the action—Jason bringing some subtle snake moves as he twists Maris around. When the bandleader calls into the mic, "Hey!" following each sung line, everyone on the dance floor calls *"Hey!"* too. The whole room is a pulsing wave of tuxes-with-jackets-shed and sequins and beaded necklaces and velvet and high-heeled pumps and stamping oxfords.

Amidst it all, rising tall, is that magnificent Christmas tree sparkling in white lights.

And when the band's ragged sax takes over, sending the jazzy melody to the rafters, the Hucklebuck dance keeps going. In the dim lighting, couples shimmy down low together. Men move behind their ladies, take hold of their hips and match step for kicking step.

"Wriggle like a snake, waddle like a duck," the bandleader sings. "Let's keep it going here, go! *Go!*"

Well, *go* Faye and Joel do. They get down and have fun like only good friends can. They're clapping and turning and strutting with each kick, each step. And the laughing, it's crazy as their legs jump and cross—*Hey! Hey!*—and jump and cross again. Yes, they dance with attitude now. Faye's shimmying in that black velvet dress and he's sliding his oxfords to the right.

When the song fades out, Joel's ready to keep going right into the next song. Faye, too, as they linger on the dance floor.

Except the next song *isn't* rocking.

The band's singer returns to the stage as a subtle piano intro winds through the shadows.

"We're going to slow things down now," the singer

says after the pianist plays a few melancholy bars. "Slow it down, nice and easy. Put your hands together, but this time? Put them in each *other's* arms."

Joel looks at Faye right as she looks at him. She gives a quick smile.

"We could sit this one out, Joel. If you're uncomfortable. Well. Because," she says, "you know."

"Or … we can dance," Joel tells her. "Come on, Weston," he says, opening his arms. He watches her there. In the few seconds that she hesitates, he sees her beautiful face fighting another smile. Sees her look away, then right at him. Sees her move aside a wisp of her fallen hair. Sees her walk right to him.

And feels her close in his arms now.

The lights dim as the piano intro shifts, the notes drifting along in a stirring lead-in. Now, in the really low lighting, the couples all around them are only silhouettes. The song, as it goes on, sounds vaguely familiar, but Joel can't place it. Is it a holiday song? *Auld Lang Syne?*

No. The piano notes eventually come together and head right into the tune. Right into *Bridge Over Troubled Water.*

Joel holds Faye close. They're winded from the last dance, so now? Now they barely move. Just slightly, they sway. She hooks one hand on his shoulder; he clasps her other hand as she looks past him. As they both feel the music. And slow their hearts. And breathe.

Joel tips his face down to hers, and when the singer's words speak of tears in a friend's eyes, Joel's actually surprised to see Faye's eyes glisten, too. He says nothing at first. He just tips his face closer and lightly touches beneath her eyes, then pulls her against him, gently pressing her head to his shoulder.

"Why the tears?" he quietly asks into her hair.

She doesn't look at him. They just keep slow-dancing, their faces practically cheek to cheek. "Thinking of my mom," Faye answers, her voice wistful. "Just missing her right now."

"Now?" Joel very slowly turns Faye on the dance floor. "Why?"

There's another pause as the singer goes on, his voice thick with emotion as he sings of lonely times, times when friends can't be found.

"Have you heard Elvis' version of this song?" Faye asks, her fingers entwined with Joel's as they move together with the music.

"No. I don't think so."

Faye shifts and looks at him. He leans low, their foreheads practically touching. Their bodies pressed close. "Elvis Presley was my mom's favorite—especially his rendition of this song. So hearing it now? It's making me sentimental," she admits as they slow-dance still. "Maybe it's the whole night doing it. The candlelit ceremony with little Abby's spirit there. And the music. All the *love* I'm seeing here." In the shadows, as lone piano notes float through the room, Faye swipes her eyes. "Anyway," her voice says near Joel's ear now as she shifts in his arms, "I someday hope to go to Graceland."

Joel raises his hand up her back and rests it on her neck as her face presses on his shoulder. "On your life list, maybe?" he asks as lyrics—melodic words about giving comfort in the darkness—wind through the room.

"Close," Faye's soft voice replies. "Number twenty-seven. Visit a place you've always wanted to see. That's what's on my list."

Still, they sway.

Still the singer's voice carries the words, the heartfelt thoughts about sailing on, and dreams, and needing a friend.

And still, they barely move together as Joel holds Faye in his arms.

But he shifts. And hooking a gentle finger beneath Faye's chin, he lifts her face. Her moist eyes lock onto his now. "Faye. Graceland *is* your number twenty-seven," he says, his voice serious. "You have to do it."

When she doesn't look away, Joel's hands cradle her neck. Wisps of her hair alight on his fingers as he dips his face close then … and kisses her. He feels Faye's emotion, too. Feels her intake of breath as she deepens the kiss. As his hands still embrace her neck and their kiss doesn't stop. As it deepens further, such that for him, their kiss is like one long inhale necessary to live. The kiss sails on with the song, with the music, with the low lights and shadows all blurred around them on the crowded dance floor of the Addison Boathouse.

# twenty-seven

AND THE KISS NEVER REALLY stops.

It keeps going on the dance floor.

More of it is stolen in Joel's pickup truck.

Beneath swirling snow in his yard, they kiss.

On his front porch, too.

And it continues in his bedroom.

Joel's arms move up Faye's velvet-clad back and pick her up, still kissing. Faye loops her hands behind his neck, and feels her black velvet dress bunch around her thighs as she wraps her legs around his hips. As he carries her to the bed. As he sits himself on the mattress. As she's on his lap.

With the kiss still going.

Still sitting on him, Faye bends down. Her arms reach around his back, his neck, as she dips her head into that kiss. Her hair, long undone now, sweeps forward. With the kiss, she feels Joel's arms move behind her shoulders, touch upon her velvet back, get those three buttons undone and partially unzip her black dress.

Oh, it's obvious. It's a kiss a long time coming.

A kiss neither wants to stop.

And Faye doesn't. She doesn't stop moving the whole time, either—kissing him, pressing close, nuzzling his neck. Desperate for him now. With her dress loosened, Joel holds an arm tight across her lower back and half stands, first—Faye's legs still slung around his hips, her arms around his neck. Shifting, then, he turns and lays her down on his bed.

And the kiss? It moves now.

In a relationship that *had* moved slowly? Now it's moving fast.

There are sharp intakes of breath.

There is a blur of hands.

Of grappling.

Joel lowers his mouth down her neck, to her shoulders—where he's pressed aside her now-loose velvet dress. Only a dim lantern shines on the dresser, so the room is dark. She and Joel are just two shadows atop the sheets. When Joel's kiss moves back to her face, his hands reach around her neck and tangle in her hair.

And Faye can barely catch her breath—but she doesn't stop.

Neither of them do.

Not as she lowers his suit pants and boxers.

Not as he slides off her black stockings, her panties.

Not as he moves half over her. His hands reach beneath her almost-off dress, slip down a bra strap and caress her breasts, skim over her bare skin beneath the velvet.

208

Her scant moan follows his intimate touch.

And yet, there are seconds—fleeting seconds—when he pauses.

In the muffled quiet, snowflakes tap at the windowpanes. Whispers come close.

His: *I need you, Faye.*

Hers: *Shh. Don't stop.*

In those few seconds, there is only breathing, and damp skin, and watching.

Until Faye sits up, unbuttons Joel's vest and denim shirt, and slips them off. She leaves scattered kisses, then, on his shoulder, his chest.

*"Faye."* His voice is low. *"You're sure?"* he asks. And waits in the darkness.

She looks at him, traces his whiskered face, and slightly nods. Turns for him to finish unzipping her dress, too.

After he gets off her bra and that twisted velvet dress, he lays her back down on the bed.

There's more touching, then.

Sometimes it's Joel's hands touching her body; sometimes it's his mouth—trailing her neck, her breasts, her belly.

She sighs in the dark; her back subtly arches in the night; each surprise of his tongue leaves her wanting more. Caught up in the pleasure, she takes Joel's hand in hers. Kisses their entwined fingers. Whispers his name as he brings his kiss to her mouth.

In the shadows, then, with the hush of falling snow outside, he moves fully over her.

Her legs straddle him as she feels the length of his body against hers.

As he strokes her hair.

As she clutches his shoulders, runs her hands over his back.

When he lowers his head and kisses her deeper now, she feels his hand slip behind her … pull her close.

Feels her own small gasp.

Feels their skin moist with perspiration.

Feels all of Joel in a tangle of bedsheets and shadows and husky, comforting murmurs.

Feels their kiss go on.

# *twenty-eight*

IT'S WELL AFTER MIDNIGHT AND all is quiet.

The room is dark.

The blinds are drawn.

Only that rustic lantern shines on the dresser.

Joel's eyes are closed. His breathing, deep. But he's awake. Awake and *sensing* everything around him. The shadows. The stillness. Sensing the furniture—that dresser on the far wall. His nightstand with the tall, black-shaded gooseneck lamp on it. The area rug covering the wide-planked wood floor. The brushed-silver floor lamp beside an upholstered reading chair. Another chair, a leather desk chair, pushed close to a small table stacked with books and paperwork.

Everything. Everything.

Faye beside him.

Faye beneath the sheets.

Now? Now he opens his eyes.

211

Opens his eyes and turns his head toward her—only to see her looking at him. So he reaches over and touches her face, toys with her mussed hair.

And stops when she gives a sad smile.

*"Joel,"* she whispers in the dark.

"Hey," he quietly answers, shifting on his side now.

Her voice is so soft. "Don't be mad at me," she says.

In a pause, Joel hears nothing but icy snowflakes hissing against the window. "What's the matter?" he finally asks.

Faye takes a breath. "I think I have to go home."

Nothing, then. Neither one speaks until Joel sits up, reaches over to that gooseneck lamp and switches it to low. Its black shade mutes the light. Shifting then, he turns to Faye again beneath the sheet. He lowers himself onto the mattress beside her and runs the back of his fingers over her shoulder.

"About tonight …" she begins.

"It was amazing," Joel says.

Says at the *same* time Faye's saying, "It was a mistake."

"What?" Lying side by side and facing each other, Joel squints at her. He keeps his voice low, too. "Faye, that wedding reception. The dancing, and celebrating. It meant *everything* to be there with you. And *here* with you."

Again, she takes a breath—this one trembling. "But maybe … we got caught up in it all."

"What are you saying?"

"Come on, Joel." Her words are quiet as the night. *"Everyone's* emotions were heightened there. Because, I mean … well, I've *never* been to a wedding like that. So intimate. And personal."

"And beautiful."

"And those feelings maybe, in the moment, carried over to us."

Joel says nothing, but now he sees Faye's eyes are moist.

Still, she lightly strokes his jaw. *"I don't want to ruin a great friendship,"* she whispers, then sits up and looks around.

"So don't."

Reaching to the end of the bed, Faye lifts her velvet dress off the mattress. Starts putting things on, too—her bra, the dress. But she says nothing while obviously fighting some emotion.

"Faye." Joel sits up. *"Don't* ruin it."

When her dress is on, she gets off the bed, scoops her underthings off the floor and sits in his reading chair. There, she quickly gets on the rest of her clothes— panties, stockings.

So Joel finds his boxers and suit pants and pulls them on. Next, he grabs his white tee off the floor, puts that on, then lifts his denim shirt off the mattress. *"Don't leave, Faye,"* he's saying while struggling to get into the twisted-up shirt. He whips it off, shakes it out and tries again.

There's a whirlwind, then. A blur of motion as Faye turns this way, that way. Grabs her pearl chandelier earrings off Joel's nightstand. Scoops up her clutch, too, and drops in the earrings. Sits on that upholstered chair again.

"Faye," Joel's saying as he half buttons up that denim shirt. "Just *stay.*" He opens the blinds on a window, then turns to her. "It's snowing. And … and it's late. I'll make you a tea. Or a decaf—anything you want."

"No." From the chair, Faye bends and picks up one of her ankle boots. "I really have to go," she says while tugging on the boot.

And Joel sees. Some panic is unwinding in her. Some doubt. Some realization that this didn't go to plan, maybe. And now *he's* panicked. So he walks to her. "Listen to me. It's okay, Faye. We can … I don't know." He drags a hand through his hair. Glances around. "We'll watch a movie. Whatever." Now he crouches right in front of her sitting on that chair. *"Don't go,"* he whispers. *"Stay the night, Faye."*

The room turns painfully quiet. If ever a moment were desperate, this one is. Faye's mussed blonde bangs sweep over her eyes—eyes still moist as she looks at Joel crouched there.

Crouched there and whispering, *"You're breaking my heart."*

*"Joel,"* she whispers back.

And he sees a fear on her face. "Talk to me," he implores.

"Okay." She lets out a breath. "Last night, the wedding in the barn. Oh, God," she says with a regretful smile. "It *was* beautiful. And sad … and *real*. What Derek and Vera found with each other …" Faye stops to give her eyes a quick swipe. When she speaks, her voice is almost disbelieving. "And … what? We were going to *replicate* that?"

"Yes." Placing his hands on either side of the upholstered chair, Joel boxes her in. "And what's wrong with that? Everything—*everything*—I felt these past few hours was *just* as real." As he waits for her to say the same, Faye silently looks long at him.

And seconds later, she bends out of his hold and puts on her second boot. "I don't *know* what's real anymore.

214

Those *ridiculous* blind dates I've been on," she says while tugging on the boot, then standing. "Us?"

Joel stands, too. His half-buttoned shirt hangs loose over his suit pants.

"What are the odds, Joel?" Faye's asking as she gets her clutch again and starts toward the bedroom door. "What truly are the odds of ever finding something like what we witnessed in that big old barn?"

"I did find it." His words stop her. "With you."

But Faye only looks over her shoulder and shakes her head.

*This can't be happening,* Joel thinks. He grabs his shoes, some socks and throws them on. Just like that, he's about to lose it all.

Lose Faye.

He rushes to the hallway and down the stairs after her. When she's putting on her camel coat at the front door, he says her name.

Takes her arm and turns her.

And is lost, just lost right now.

"Faye," he says, shaking his head. "You're overthinking things. You were … *happy*, earlier. You *had* no doubts. Just go with what you feel. What you *felt*." His hands, they hold her arms. *"Want."*

For a long moment, there's some hope. Some possibility. Until she whispers to him.

*"I'm sorry, Joel. It's not you. Please believe me."*

"I can't. Not this—that you're *leaving.*"

Faye backs up a step, then.

When she does, he lets go of her arms. Turns up his hands.

215

"It's me, Joel. It's all me," she says. After swiping at another tear, she clutches her coat tightly closed and heads out the door.

"Faye!" Joel follows her to the porch and turns her again. It's cold out. A wind's picked up, too. So right away Joel feels icy snowflakes on his face. "It's *snowing*, Faye," he says to her at his porch step. "Let me at least drive you."

She shakes her head no. That's it. Shakes her head, turns, bends into the wind and walks away.

Joel just stands there in his wrinkled suit pants and loose shirt. Beside the porch, colored lights on the tall fir tree glimmer in the night.

Still he just stands and watches Faye trudge through the snowy yard to her bungalow next door.

# twenty-nine

THERE'S A NOISE.

Lying in her bed Sunday morning, Faye listens.

The noise doesn't wake her up, though. Because it's not like she even slept last night. No, her thoughts made sure of that.

Thoughts tapping at her conscience.

Thoughts tossing and turning her beneath the blanket.

Thoughts keeping her eyes wide open in the dark.

Thoughts bringing her to a window to look at Joel's farmhouse next door.

Thoughts leading her to pick up her cell phone, find his name in the contacts, look at it through some stinging tears, then put the phone down again.

Thoughts reminding her how *wonderful* the night had been with Joel.

How freeing.

And thoughts of the what-ifs now.

*What if I simply fell under the spell of an enchanted night?* she wonders.

*Or what if I seriously fell ... for Joel? For dear, sweet Joel.*

But that noise—it distracts her. So she puts on her slippers and robe and heads to the living room window. And for a moment, her eyes drop closed.

But just for a moment.

Just until she opens them to the snowy sight outside—and to Joel, too. Wearing his wool cap and a dark parka, he's shoveling her driveway. Scraping that shovel beneath a swath of fluffy snow and sliding it off to the side. Again, and again.

Faye swallows a hard knot in her throat as she watches. Because that's Joel Briggs for you. Taking care of everyone. His patrons in the tavern with his Trouble Tree lightening their worries. And with his whisk brooms sweeping away the bad. Taking care of his family with an undoubtedly sweet Thanksgiving. Taking care of townsfolk, too, making sure they have some Friday fun at bingo night.

*And* looking after her—his neighbor. Being sure she can get her car out today.

Or is he doing something else? Is he just letting her know everything's all right? Not to worry about the night before, come what may?

Joel's about finished with the driveway—she sees that. He's moving to the stone walkway leading to her front entry alcove. In no time, that's cleared, too. So she brushes back her no-sleep, tossing-and-turning-mussed-hair and hurries to her front door. Opens it, too, right as he's turning to leave.

"Thanks, Joel," she calls out, standing there and

218

holding her robe closed. "You didn't have to do all that."

"Well," he calls back over his shoulder. "You're all set now," he says, waving and walking away.

Faye just leans in the open doorway and watches. A few leftover snowflakes drop from the cloudy sky. Her yard is blanketed in white. There's a muffled quiet in the air.

Still she watches Joel walk to his farmhouse next door.

And almost calls out to him again. She actually half steps out, arm raised. But sadly stops herself.

So you see? What started with one unexpected kiss on the dance floor last night—and now they can't even talk.

❧

Things aren't any better Monday—just one week before Christmas.

*Maybe they're worse,* Faye thinks when she shows up for an appointment at a client's restaurant and finds she brought the wrong flatware samples in her wheelie-office.

Thinks it again back at Silver Settings when she disconnects a call while transferring it to another associate.

And again when she forgets about an afternoon marketing meeting in the conference room and is ten minutes late—sweeping in all flustered.

Thinks it again Monday night when she gets two paper cuts wrapping Christmas gifts in front of the TV—while keeping an eye to the window facing a certain farmhouse next door, too.

❧

It's been a rough Monday.

Still, Joel figures he'd rather be at the tavern than sitting home.

Earlier, he'd forgotten to deliver a customer's lunch order to the kitchen—until the impatient customer reminded him fifteen minutes later.

He dropped some coins, too, when giving change to another customer.

And this evening, Joel pours the wrong drink—twice.

Then he tallies the wrong amount for *another* customer and has to re-ring the entire order.

"What's eating you, Briggs?" Kevin finally asks during a lull in the evening.

"Nothing. Just busy." Joel swipes a damp rag over the bar. "It's the week before Christmas, you know? Have a lot on my mind."

Kevin eyes him. "It's that woman, isn't it?"

Joel gives a short laugh, then reluctantly sits himself on the stool at the Trouble Tree. It's all a-glimmer with twinkling white lights shining on boughs *full* of glittered mini bells. Troubles, it seems, hang from every branch.

Kevin walks over and lifts a green bell from a nearby basket. Handing the bell to Joel, he tells him, "Lay it on me, Briggs."

And Joel does. He toys with that glitter ornament as he tells Kevin all about the girl next door. And a little about his broken heart, too, before hanging his own mini bell on the illuminated Trouble Tree.

Tuesday's a repeat of Monday—troubled.

Late morning, Joel cancels his Friday night bingo gig. It's the last one before Christmas, with all sorts of festive games planned. But he's just not feeling it. The holiday spirit eludes him, so he phones his friend Arthur to cover his bingo night.

After talking to Arthur, Joel decides to go for a trail run. First, he downloads a song to listen to while running. Of course, it's Elvis' rendition of *Bridge Over Troubled Water*. A light coating of snow dusts the paved trail winding through the woods. But Joel wears his lug-sole sneakers and goose-down vest, fleece-lined gloves and wool beanie, so he's good.

Good to pound his worries out *on* that pavement.

*And* listen to the song that brought Faye to tears at the wedding reception.

But hearing the lyrics while running, Joel wonders. What *really* brought Faye to tears Saturday night when the band played the song? Because listening closely now, that song *could* describe *them*, actually—starting from last New Year's Eve when he stopped her sad tears, straight through all these months when she sailed right into her dreams, and got her cherished bungalow, and started her new job, and fully lived her life list.

And he sailed along right with her—a friend through it all—hearing every detail, every moment of those dreams.

Still running now, Joel notices a large stick—more a small limb—fallen across the trail up ahead. So he stops at it, picks it up, jostles it in his hands some.

Then? For all he's worth, he whips that branch

crashing through the brush, sending it deep, deep into the woods.

⁓O

Tuesday evening, Faye sits in her father's kitchen. Miniature wreaths hang from long ribbons over the cabinet fronts. A small Christmas tree made from curls of birch bark is in the kitchen window. Her father fried pork chops and onions, and they're just sitting down to eat together. This time, though, is different from other chatty evenings when they've had supper like this.

This time, Faye's subdued.

She can't even help it, the way words don't come.

There's only the click of forks and knives on their plates, and a few phrases spoken here and there. Her father asking about Derek and Vera's wedding. She asking when her father's off teaching for Christmas break.

Then, nothing.

Nothing until her father asks, "You okay, Faye? You seem quiet."

"I'm fine," she tells him with a quick smile. "Really, Dad." She stabs a piece of pork chop, drags it through applesauce on her plate, and looks across the table at him. "Oh, heck," she says, then lifts that forked pork chop piece to her mouth. "I can't lie to you."

"I knew it." Her father sets down *his* fork and leans on his elbows. "What's wrong, Faye?"

"Huh." She sips some sparkling water, then slowly spins the glass on the table. "In a word?" She looks over at him. "Everything."

And it's more of the same on Wednesday morning.

More of Faye opening her heart at a table. Well, at the soda fountain at Dane's General Store, actually. She called Sadie from work and asked if she could meet her for a coffee break.

Now they're sitting on stools at the counter and sipping butterscotch caramel coffees topped with whipped cream and sprinkled with cinnamon. And talking. Around them, the general store is just dripping Christmas. There are ornament displays. And a copper trough filled with pine-scented candles. Gift baskets of candies. Rolls of wrapping paper and bags of bows. A row of toys, a rack of holiday cards. Twinkling lights strung along the rafters, too. And shoppers galore.

"That was some kiss on the dance floor Saturday," Sadie is saying, lowering her steaming coffee mug at the counter. "Between you and Joel."

Faye nods and holds her coffee close. Sips it, too, before going on. "The kiss didn't end on the dance floor, Sadie," she quietly admits.

"I didn't think so."

Then? Then Faye tells a little different version of her story to Sadie.

A version different from what she told her father the day before.

A version you only tell a good friend.

A version about going home with Joel after Vera and Derek's wedding.

And Sadie hangs on her every word. And nods. And squeezes Faye's hand.

*"Our friendship turned into something else that night,"* Faye nearly whispers. "But into what, I'm not sure yet. So is it the best thing that ever happened—or the absolute worst?"

"What? Why?"

"Sadie, we had such a good thing going, me and Joel. We were *friends*. But now?"

"Now *what?*"

"Now I feel like I ruined everything."

"Faye. Don't say that."

"I just got so afraid after we slept together. Said some things I wish I hadn't. And I … I left. Just went home. And I regret that now. Because I really hurt him."

*"Oh no, Faye."*

Faye nods. "And we haven't talked since—which worries me. Because these past few weeks? We've had some *amazing* talks, Sadie. So did I lose my friend? Will we even talk again?"

"You *have* to."

"All I know, Sadie, is that Saturday night at the wedding? And at Joel's house afterward? When it was all actually happening? Everything just felt … right."

Wednesday night, Joel thinks he'll leave the lights off on the towering fir tree in his yard. Well, he thinks it for about a minute and a half. Thinks it until he sees two cars slowly drive past his farmhouse—and he knows. They're looking for his tree. Looking for some Christmas spirit. For a smile. For something majestic in the night.

So he turns on the tree lights, then grabs his jacket and hat and goes out on the front porch. The night is cold and clear. Tiny stars twinkle like white Christmas lights in the sky above. His grand fir tree drops a glow on the snow-dusted lawn.

And next door at Faye's house? Her Christmas tree—the one they bought together—shines in her living room window. So she's home.

He crosses his arms and leans on a porch post. Looks longer at Faye's country bungalow. The dark silhouettes of tall trees rise in a thicket behind it. Some of her windows glow with lamplight.

So Joel steps off his porch and starts to walk there. But halfway, he veers off. Circles around to his rock wall, then heads back to his front porch.

And won't look toward Faye's house again. Because if he does, he'll end up going there. End up ringing her doorbell. And saying stilted phrases. *Faye. About last weekend. I don't know, something happened. Let's talk. Or walk.*

And would she walk? And talk? Or would she say she's busy? Or that Saturday night shouldn't have happened? Or would she just give a sad smile and shake her head?

Well, by looking away, he won't be tempted to go there.

Won't intrude on whatever's bothering her. Or holding her back.

Standing still in the night, though, he hears it. The barred owls are calling.

*Who-who. Who-whoo.*

In the distance, another throaty, muffled call answers. *Who-who ... Who-whoo.*

Are they telling him something, those owls? *Just-let. Her-go … Just-let. Her-go.*

Joel looks to the black sky. Watches for a swooping shadow of one of those night eagles.

But is only left with their faint echo in the darkness.

# *thirty*

His DECISION'S MADE.

Thursday morning, after another sleepless night, Joel's mind is made up.

He *will* let Faye Weston go—if this one last plea doesn't work.

Because he knows. Once they finally stopped denying their feelings for each other—something got her to run. Was it her own heart that did it—catching her so off guard? Was it the difficult past she mentioned to him on that tree bench? He doesn't know.

But he's also willing to do what it takes to find out.

So after showering, and putting on his black pants and vest over white button-down for work, and having some breakfast, he heads out.

But before getting to his tavern, he makes one stop.

He parks in front of a big yellow colonial on Main Street. It's the historic 1700s Chapman House, now home to many town offices. One of which is the office of Addison's event planner—Sadie Wells.

Joel goes inside, checks the lobby directory and finds Sadie's room number. He clears his throat, walks down a hallway and stops at her open office. Sadie's at her desk and immersed in something at her computer. Beyond her, paned windows look out onto Main Street storefronts all decorated with garland and lights for the holidays. Just then, the Holly Trolley jingles past, too.

But Joel looks to Sadie now and gives a one-two knock on the doorframe.

"Joel!" Sadie says, looking up from her work. She sets down a pen and turns her wheeled chair toward him. "Can I help you with something?"

"Yeah." He pulls off his wool beanie and walks into her office. "I really hope you can."

✧

After work Thursday evening, Faye changes into a loose fisherman sweater, black leggings and sherpa-lined slipper socks. It's cold out, and so she's staying in for the night. Dinner and a movie will pass the time. With her supper, she opens a few Christmas cards that came in the mail. Afterward, she goes to the living room and switches on her Christmas tree at the picture window. She stands there for a minute, too, and looks outside.

Looks across the yard to Joel's farmhouse. Lamplight glows in the windows; his pickup is parked in the driveway. So he's home. In his front yard, his towering fir tree is glimmering in the dark. Colored lights shine beneath snow still on the boughs. It's a beautiful sight, one that enchants her every night.

And when her cell phone rings just then, Faye scoops it off an end table and hopes it *is* Joel.

It's not.

"Hey, Faye," Sadie says. "Just checking to be sure you got my email."

"Email?"

"For your last Merry Match date tomorrow. I never got your confirmation."

"What?" Faye scrolls the emails on her phone. "There's nothing here. And I thought Luca was the last date."

"No, there were five. One more tomorrow. It's all arranged the way you'd requested—at Joel's tavern."

"No way, Sadie. I can't set foot there now." Faye sinks into a tufted-back, overstuffed chair. A chair facing her paned picture window giving a clear view to Joel's farmhouse. "After everything I told you?" Faye goes on. "It doesn't feel right."

"I know, and I'm sorry, but—"

"I don't even know where Joel and I stand," Faye interrupts. "And I *don't* want to hurt his feelings going in there for another date, either."

"But the arrangements are already made."

"And my heart's just not in it. I even cancelled things with Luca. So can't we let Merry Match go?"

"Oh, Faye." Sadie pauses, then softly goes on. "It's late. I'd have to do a *lot* of chasing to cancel now. *And* I'm not in the office, where all the names and phone numbers are."

"Fine. I don't want to put you in a predicament, so ..."

"Okay, good. I'll resend your email from work tomorrow—with all the details. Your date's meeting you at Joel's at seven o'clock, but you *can* leave together right away. You know … go to the coffee shop if that's easier. And didn't you say Joel doesn't work nights anyway? He might not even be there."

"Maybe." Faye walks back to her illuminated Christmas tree now. She stands there and looks out across the dark yard. "Listen, Sadie. No worries. I'll just handle it."

# *thirty-one*

FRIDAY EVENING, FAYE KEEPS THINGS simple. She wears a simple black turtleneck sweater with skinny jeans and her black Chelsea boots. She arrives at Joel's Bar and Grille on time, too. Doesn't alter her simple routine. She just walks into the dark tavern and crosses the wide-planked wood floor to her regular table.

Oh, she glances around, though. And is relieved that Joel isn't here. But she checks with Kevin—just to be sure.

"Joel here?" she casually calls to him at the bar.

"No, not right now," Kevin says.

So at her table, Faye keeps to her routine. Takes off her gold-plaid coat and drapes it on her chairback. Adjusts her chair to just the right angle. Sits then, too.

And clears her throat.

And watches the six-panel black wooden door.

And looks over to Kevin at the bar.

"Not too busy tonight," she mentions.

"It's early still," he tells her while stacking clean wineglasses. "But folks'll pile in for our renowned Christmas charades later."

"*Christmas.* Just a few days away now."

"Yep." Kevin waves to a patron leaving, then says to Faye from the bar, "Another Merry Match date tonight?"

"Anytime now." She glances at her watch, then checks her phone for a late email from Sadie. None have arrived all day, so Faye knows *nothing* about her date—not even his name. She quickly texts Sadie a reminder, then sets her phone aside.

"How've the dates been going, anyway?" Kevin asks, wiping the bar down now.

"Oh, you know." Faye shifts her chair some. "Okay."

Kevin nods before turning to a customer approaching the bar.

And Faye looks around. The tavern's quiet. The jukebox is off. People sit at some tables. Couples. Friends. A few guys hang out at the bar and talk with Kevin. The place is fully decorated, too. Red neon bells flash in the front window. The flocked Christmas tree near the door twinkles in the shadows. The little Trouble Tree does, too. Garland loops; mistletoe hangs; birch deer stand at either end of the bar.

But still no date.

Faye checks her watch again just as someone opens that big wooden door.

And her heart drops when she sees it's Joel. His navy duffle coat hangs loose, the toggle buttons unfastened. Beneath it he wears a V-neck sweater over a flannel shirt, jeans and chukka boots—not his standard black pants and vest with white button-down.

So he's not here to work.

And he's heading her way.

"How you doing, Faye?" he asks. "One more date tonight?"

"Oh, Joel." She clears her throat and sits up straight. "Sorry. I mean, I'm *really* sorry. It feels funny being here after ... Well, there was a mix-up with Sadie. For this last date." Faye gives him an apologetic smile. "She couldn't change the location at the last minute, so when he arrives ..." Faye pauses and looks to the door. And hopes, prays, wishes it would just open. That her date would arrive so she could leave.

But the door stays closed. No one's arriving.

So she looks at Joel standing there at her table. He must not have shaved for a few days, so his face is scruffy. And his dark hair curls from beneath his beanie—which he pulls off just then. "Well," Faye manages to tell him. "When this guy arrives, we'll take off for somewhere else."

Joel watches her. And gives a shrug. "It's okay. Really," he says, then crosses that planked floor to the bar. When he returns, he's holding the Merry Match candy-cane heart figurine and sets it on her table. He pulls out a chair and sits there, too. "You don't have to worry about it, Faye. Because I'm your date tonight."

⌒⌒〇

"You're my ... *what?*" Faye asks, staring at him.

"Your date." Joel reaches over and shakes her hand. "Joel Briggs."

A quick, and easy, smile comes to Faye's face. "What are you doing, Joel?"

"Giving us another shot." He leans back and snaps his fingers to Kevin then.

"Wait," Faye says. "Sadie arranged … *this?*"

"Yesterday." Joel looks at Faye across the table. At beautiful Faye, with her blunt blonde hair just reaching her shoulders. With her gold hoop earrings glimmering. With her disbelieving smile. And maybe some tears in her eyes. "Sadie set this up," Joel explains, leaning close over the table, "after I just about begged her to."

"You really did that? You talked to her?"

Joel nods.

Faye sits back in her chair and scrutinizes him. Kevin approaches, too. He sets down two glasses of wine, then lights a candle in a red globe at their table. Gives a knowing wink to Faye, too. When he returns to the bar, he dims the lights in the tavern.

And Faye smiles in a way that tells Joel something— between that smile and her moist eyes. She's okay with this.

"Listen." Joel takes off his coat and sets it on another chair. He also scrapes *his* chair closer to Faye's. In the quiet bar, he keeps his voice low, too. "Last New Year's, when I told you to hold your tears? Because crying on New Year's brings on a year of sadness? I thought about you afterward. But I didn't know your name. Didn't know who you were. Still … I wondered if things worked out for you." As he talks, Joel sees how Faye's eyes are locked onto his. She struggles with some emotion, too—but in a good way. There's happiness, there. "Anyway," Joel goes

234

on, folding his flannel shirtsleeves back over his sweater, "then I had to forget you because … that was it. You were in and out of here, and I never saw you again. Life moved on. But now?" He reaches over, takes her hand and clasps it in both of his. "Now I can't stop thinking about you."

Faye looks away—then right back at him. *"Me, too,"* she whispers. *"About you."*

The thing is, as she says it, she's nodding. And more tears rise.

*"Shh,"* Joel whispers, dabbing a tear on her face.

Faye puts a hand over her mouth like she just can't talk right now.

Joel reads her eyes, though. And sees the smile in them, too. "Faye," he says. "Before anything else, I want to say something about what happened Saturday night. About you leaving."

"Joel. I'm so sorry I—"

"No, please. I know you're working through things. I know it hasn't been an easy year." Joel sits back in his chair. The tavern is shadowed. Coach-light sconces flicker on the dark paneled walls. An oil painting of a schooner at sea hangs near their table. And Joel looks only at Faye when he goes on, his voice serious. "I also know something went down in your last relationship." Now? Now he turns up his hands. "But I'm not him."

*"No,"* Faye whispers back. "You're not … Oh, Joel." She slowly shakes her head, obviously at a loss for words—but not for long. "Thank you," she says.

"For what?"

"For your patience. Things in my life kind of went differently than I'd thought." A stalled moment falls between them. *"And I just hope it's not too late for us,"* Faye quietly admits in the shadows.

"Well." He leans forward and rests his arms on the table. "Let's get on with this blind date and we'll see, okay? See if we're a match."

Faye nods. And shifts in her chair. And watches him.

"Now ... you don't have to tell me all about yourself, Faye." Before going on, Joel pauses to sip his wine. "Because I want to tell *you* all the things I *already* know about you."

Faye leans to him and strokes his whiskered jaw. Her fingers tremble as they trace his chin and move briefly to his hair, his neck.

*"You're very particular,"* his low voice begins. *"And like things ... just so."*

She slightly smiles.

"Your amazing meatloaf." He kisses his pinched-together fingertips. "Your Christmas tree perfectly centered in your living room window."

Still, Faye just watches him. But that smile stays, too.

So he keeps going. "You've *found* your decorating style—hipstoric. And ... And your job? Well, you're *so* dedicated to it, making sure families have beautiful memories around the table. I know you also care deeply about your *own* family, and that I've never seen your father happier since you moved back to town." Joel pauses. "And your smile?" he asks, touching her face. "It lights up a room—heck, even a grocery store aisle."

When she starts to talk, Joel raises his hand. "A few more first?" When she nods, he goes on. "You like to sit on your stoop at night."

Listening still, Faye sits back. "To hear the night eagles," she adds.

"And talk." Joel tips his head, watching her. "Let's see. You cook a mean peanut butter blossom cookie. You're an early bird, too. And … January is your favorite month, because of the hope of it."

He pauses when she nods again—briefly squeezing her eyes shut this time.

"And I know that you don't like to travel far from home, Faye, unless it's for a special reason."

Funny, but Joel notices something *else*, too. He notices how the whole bar's gone quiet around them.

But he goes on. "And you *do* have a special reason to travel," he says, looking only at her. At her beautiful eyes loving every bit of this. "Number twenty-seven on your life list. Visit Graceland, some place you've always wanted to see. Hopefully with me, okay? But you *also* love staying in and watching movies. And I definitely know that you have the *best* handwriting." He takes a few seconds to just look at her. To tuck back a wisp of her hair. *"You're pretty darn good with a sewing needle, too,"* he whispers close. And leans even closer, still whispering. *"And maybe you were afraid Saturday night. Afraid it wasn't real. Afraid we were caught up in the night."* He pauses now. Pauses to get past an emotional knot in *his* throat. "But here's the thing, Faye," he manages. "I didn't get caught up in the night. I'm caught up in you."

Now? More tears streak Faye's face.

*"Hey, it's okay,"* he softly says, lightly brushing those tears away. "And I'm going to tell you *one* thing you *don't* know about me."

"What?" she barely asks.

"That I fell in love with the girl next door."

"Joel," she begins, but he stops her.

"I love you, Faye Weston. And I actually may have since last New Year's Eve."

"Joel," she says again.

"What is it, sweetheart?"

Again, a smile. "I worried." She takes a shaking breath in the shadowed, dimly lit bar. "At first, I wondered if this could work," she says, motioning between them. "And what would happen if it didn't. But now? Now I'm more afraid of *losing* you than anything else."

"That's never going to happen, and here's why." Joel moves his chair closer—as close as he can get to her. He raises his hands and cradles her neck, too. "Because you're the best *friend* I'll ever have."

He kisses her, then. Right there in the tavern. Right there with the few patrons privy to this whole scene. He kisses her, once, twice, until she deepens that kiss, and murmurs into it, and smiles beneath it, too.

When she pulls away, she touches his face, his hair. *"I love you, too,"* she whispers, and kisses him again—as he wraps an arm around her shoulders and pulls her even closer—all as some whistles ring out behind them, and a sporadic round of cheers and applause fills the dark tavern.

238

# *thirty-two*

A DREAM, A BEAUTIFUL DREAM.

That's what Faye feels like she's in. A dream where she looks up at the sky and is in a snow globe. Snowflakes swirl down, alighting on her face. She feels each one's delicate touch on her skin.

But she's not in a dream. Sunday afternoon, she's sitting on her favorite tree bench at the little green on Winter Road. The painted bench encircles the wide trunk of a tall maple tree. Wearing her black cable-knit poncho and gold beret, Faye leans against the bench's slatted back.

It's Christmas Eve day.

Balsam wreaths hang on the doors of neighboring homes—Tudors and colonials. White lights already twinkle on hedges and picket fences.

There's also that Christmas Eve hush in the air. That time when the whole earth seems to pause and let something else take over.

Hope. Solemnity. Love.

Sitting on that tree bench, Faye pauses, too. And takes stock of where she's landed this year—in her cherished country bungalow. Right here on Winter Road. She thinks of the special job she began at Silver Settings. And of a particular tavern owner.

She thinks of Joel.

Thinks of every moment they've spent together in the few days since their blind date. The Christmas movies they watched. The meals they ate. The talks they had. The touches. The emotion.

As she thinks, the snow keeps falling around her. Tiny white flakes—soft and silent. In a moment, she reaches into her satchel and finds her new mini magnifying glass. That magnifier almost feels like a mirror reflecting back her own life. Because she feels the *same* wonder looking at a glistening snowflake on her arm as she's felt since Friday night—when Joel Briggs set that candy-cane heart figurine on her table and said he was her date.

Since then, yes. Her life's been as beautiful as *every* delicate snowflake drifting and spinning from the cloudy sky right now in some magical Christmas waltz.

⌒❦〇

Christmas Eve, Joel closes the tavern early.

As the last of his patrons cross the planked floor, slip into coats and hats, and head to the door, lingering holiday wishes ring out. Joel waves and returns the same good cheer to those who stopped in for merry greetings, a bite to eat, a holiday toast. When the last couple takes off, Joel holds open the six-panel wood door and wishes them well. Outside, snow is falling in the misty light of the colonial-style lampposts. Last-minute shoppers holding bags stuffed with gifts hurry past on the cobblestone sidewalk. They smile and call out to him. Someone's taking a snowy sleigh ride around the town green. Bells on the horse's harness jingle with its every trotted step.

Joel takes a long look, then puts out the *Closed* sign and locks up. Behind him in the tavern, Kevin's wiping down the bar.

"Where's Faye this Christmas Eve?" he asks, moving that damp rag around the Trouble Tree now.

"At her aunt's." Joel walks to the framed oil paintings on the walls and turns off the brass picture lamps above them. "We made plans for tomorrow."

"You'll miss her tonight."

"That I will."

After the bar's scrubbed, Kevin dries a few cleaned glasses. "What about your family?" he asks Joel. "Your folks, your brother—they around?"

"Seeing them tomorrow, too." Joel shoves up his white shirtsleeves and heads to the register behind the bar. "Listen, guy. Why don't you take off now?"

"You sure?" Kevin asks. "I usually close up."

"My night's quiet. You get home to your wife. Oh, and one more thing," Joel says while reaching to a shelf beneath the register. He lifts a festive Merry Market gift bag and gives it to Kevin. "Happy holidays, Kev. You have a good one."

"Hey, man. You, too," Kevin tells him when he takes the gift. "Christmas cheers, Joel."

Once Kevin grabs his coat and heads out the door, Joel finishes up alone. Shadows grow long on the tavern's paneled walls. The jukebox glows, but is quiet. He crosses the wood-planked floor. Wipes down all the tables with a damp rag. That done, he also straightens every Windsor chair at each table. One at a time he nudges a chair here, there, getting every one of them … just so. He sweeps, too. The broom bristles brush over crumbs and dust—each sweep of those bristles like some clock ticking away the seconds.

There's only the sound of his footsteps then, his tidying up, in the still tavern.

The sound of him cashing out the register.

Of putting away more cleaned glasses.

Of straightening a few bottles of liquor on the shelf behind the bar.

Of moving the latest basket of whisk brooms his parents dropped off for New Year's.

Of getting his coat and locking up his office door.

Finally, it's time to head home. At the black-painted entrance door, he dims all the lights in the tavern—but leaves on the blinking neon bells in the front window. Giving a last look behind him before stepping outside, Joel's gaze stops longest at one particular table.

The one angled with a view toward the door.

The table where a gold-plaid coat hung over a certain chairback many nights these past few weeks.

The table that changed his life.

With a smile then, he slips on his beanie and duffle coat before walking alone out into the night.

Traffic's light driving home. Shops are closed up. On Addison's cobblestone walkways, carolers in historical costumes hold lanterns and sing holiday hymns. The carolers' voices rise in the still night. Arched windows of the white-steepled chapel are aglow for evening services.

Joel sees it all, driving through town.

When he finally turns onto Winter Road, it's a welcome sight. All the homes—the farmhouses and Tudors and saltboxes—are blanketed in snow. Tiny lights on shrubs and strung around lampposts glimmer beneath that white dusting. He can see inside some of the houses—chandelier-lit dining rooms where families mingle; living rooms where people gather around garland-lined fireplaces. Friends and relatives park in driveways, then walk the snowy paths to front doors adorned with balsam wreaths blowing in a light wind.

Finally, he sees his farmhouse ahead. The split-rail fence running beside it is capped with white snow. More snow gloves the bare branches of the maple tree near his house. Shrubs beside his porch hang heavy beneath the snow's weight. And on the boughs of his tall fir tree, the strung colored lights are mere smudges of red, green and gold beneath that snow. Wall lanterns mounted on the open porch cast a glow on it all.

He parks in the driveway, but before heading inside, looks over at Faye's bungalow. She's still not home; her house is dark in the night. Turning then, Joel walks up his driveway toward his front porch. His footsteps are muffled in the fresh-fallen snow. Walking along, though, a motion catches his eye. It gets him to stop and squint through the evening's shadows.

It's Faye.

So he stands there, beside his towering fir tree, and watches. She's bundled up in her warm coat, beret and gloves. And she's doing something. It looks like she's using one of the tavern's mini whisk brooms to sweep snow off the stoop. When she's done, she spreads a plaid blanket on the top step. And sits. Right there. And snuggles into that gold-plaid coat.

Joel looks at her, and at his farmhouse, and at his illuminated, snow-laden tree in the yard. He glances at the silvery-gray sky, too, and gives a nod of gratitude before walking in Faye's direction.

"Hey. What are you doing here?" he asks at the front steps. "I thought you were going to your aunt's."

"I was there with my father for a while." Faye smiles and pats the stoop for him. "But I left early."

Joel sits beside her on the top step. He puts an arm around her shoulders, leans in and kisses the side of her head. "Why'd you leave so soon, though?"

Faye looks at him. "To be with *you*." She kisses him, too. Just a breath of a kiss, her lips brushing his. Her fingers tracing his whiskered jaw. "On Christmas."

He doesn't know what it is then, but his emotion gets to him. Sitting with Faye, he leans his arms on his knees and drops his head. Then looks back at her sitting there. At her beautiful hazel eyes watching him from beneath her sweeping bangs. At snowflakes dusting her coat, her beret.

*"I love you,"* she quietly says in the dark of night, with his towering tree glimmering in the yard. *"So very much."*

And he chokes up with the truth of it all. With Faye. With what he's feeling.

But he hides it, that knot in his throat, as he looks back at her.

As she whispers his name.

As he tells her he's *so* glad she's here.

As they hear a barred owl's soft call in the holy night.

As light snowflakes drift from the sky.

It's a moment Joel Briggs never saw coming—not once during this entire, livelong year.

A moment that brings him to tears.

*"Oh, Joel,"* Faye whispers again, leaving a kiss on his face. Just one. "Like you told me last New Year's Eve, hold those tears back," she softly goes on. "Because … legend has it that you'll be doomed to a very sad *Christmas* otherwise." As she says it, as she sits there, her fingers trace his hair. And stroke his jaw.

Watching her so near, he briefly closes his disbelieving eyes—until feeling her feather kiss on them. With that, he looks at her again.

And keeps those tears in check.

And puts an arm around Faye's shoulders to hold her close on the porch stoop.

Close enough that they press near—their bodies touching, their words few.

Close enough that they look together out at the snowy yards … and at wintry trees where night eagles perch unseen.

Close enough that Joel might otherwise have missed the words Faye barely whispers in the dark, cold night.

*"Merry Christmas, my dear friend."*

# ENJOY MORE OF
# THE WINTER NOVELS

1) Snowflakes and Coffee Cakes

2) Snow Deer and Cocoa Cheer

3) Cardinal Cabin

4) First Flurries

5) Eighteen Winters

6) Winter House

7) Winter Road

— And more Winter Novels —

FROM NEW YORK TIMES BESTSELLING AUTHOR

# JOANNE DEMAIO

# *Also by Joanne DeMaio*

# Also by Joanne DeMaio

**The Seaside Saga**
(In order)
1) *Blue Jeans and Coffee Beans*
2) *The Denim Blue Sea*
3) *Beach Blues*
4) *Beach Breeze*
5) *The Beach Inn*
6) *Beach Bliss*
7) *Castaway Cottage*
8) *Night Beach*
9) *Little Beach Bungalow*
10) *Every Summer*
11) *Salt Air Secrets*
12) *Stony Point Summer*
13) *The Beachgoers*
14) *Shore Road*
15) *The Wait*
16) *The Goodbye*
17) *The Barlows*
18) *The Visitor*
19) *Stairway to the Sea*
20) *The Liars*
*–And More Seaside Saga Books–*

For a complete list of books by *New York Times*
bestselling author Joanne DeMaio, visit:

Joannedemaio.com

# About the Author

JOANNE DEMAIO is a *New York Times* and *USA Today* bestselling author of contemporary fiction. The novels of her ongoing and groundbreaking Seaside Saga journey with a group of beach friends, much the way a TV series does, continuing with the same cast of characters from book-to-book. In addition, she writes winter novels set in a quaint New England town. Joanne lives with her family in Connecticut.

For a complete list of books and for news on upcoming releases, visit Joanne's website. She also enjoys hearing from readers on Facebook.

**Author Website:**
Joannedemaio.com

**Facebook:**
Facebook.com/JoanneDeMaioAuthor